The warmth she'd seen in his eyes disappeared, and she told herself it shouldn't matter. It was better they remember who they were to each other— people who had a troubled girl in common but nothing more.

She couldn't allow it to be anything more.

"You need a Christmas tree," he said as she started to back away.

"I didn't see any decorations in your house."

He nodded. "Yeah, but Stella made me promise I would at least get a tree."

"I'll consider a tree," Madison told him. It felt like a small concession. "Although I'm not much for Christmas spirit."

"That makes two of us."

Once again, she wasn't sure how to feel about having something in common with Chase.

Dear Reader,

I'm so excited to share *Starlight and the Christmas Dare* with you. There is something special about writing (and reading) a holiday romance, and the town of Starlight is particularly charming at this time of year.

Madison Maurer and Chase Kent are going to need all the extra charm and Christmas magic they can find in their path to happily-ever-after. Neither of them believes in love or miracles, but they join forces to help a troubled teenage girl cope with the loss of her parents. By helping Stella rediscover the wonder and joy of the season, Chase and Madison might just find it for themselves as well.

I hope this holiday season brings you much joy. To keep up with me, you can sign up for my newsletter at www.michellemajor.com, or find me on Facebook or Instagram.

Happy reading and big hugs!

Michelle

Starlight and the Christmas Dare

MICHELLE MAJOR

HARLEQUIN

SPECIAL
EDITION

ISBN-13: 978-1-335-72432-8

Starlight and the Christmas Dare

Copyright © 2022 by Michelle Major

For questions and comments about the quality of this book,
please contact us at CustomerService@Harlequin.com.

Harlequin Enterprises ULC
22 Adelaide St. West, 41st Floor
Toronto, Ontario M5H 4E3, Canada
www.Harlequin.com

Printed in U.S.A.

Michelle Major grew up in Ohio but dreamed of living in the mountains. Soon after graduating with a degree in journalism, she pointed her car west and settled in Colorado. Her life and house are filled with one great husband, two beautiful kids, a few furry pets and several well-behaved reptiles. She's grateful to have found her passion writing stories with happy endings. Michelle loves to hear from her readers at michellemajor.com.

Books by Michelle Major

Harlequin Special Edition

Welcome to Starlight

The Best Intentions
The Last Man She Expected
His Secret Starlight Baby
Starlight and the Single Dad
A Starlight Summer

Maggie & Griffin

Falling for the Wrong Brother
Second Chance in Stonecreek
A Stonecreek Christmas Reunion

The Fortunes of Texas: The Wedding Gift

Their New Year's Beginning

The Fortunes of Texas: The Hotel Fortune

Her Texas New Year's Wish

The Fortunes of Texas: Rambling Rose

Fortune's Fresh Start

Visit the Author Profile page
at Harlequin.com for more titles.

For my mom and dad,
for years of family Christmas fun.

Chapter One

Chase Kent stood in the mist of the early December night and stared at the window across the street from the alley that kept him hidden from view.

He'd lived in Seattle for half his life and thought he was immune to the damp winter cold, but at the moment, he felt frigid to his bones. It was as much outright terror as anything else.

The door to the youth center opened, and his teenage stepsister walked out with two boys who looked to be her age. Had one of those kids gotten them into this current mess, and what would happen if he went over and confronted the little punk?

They were taller than Stella, who took after her

mother, Chase's late stepmom. Her small, nearly elfin size might make Stella tiny in stature, but she was a powerhouse of attitude.

One of the kids offered her a cigarette as they walked toward the light-rail station. Chase held his breath, wondering if she would accept it, then muttered a prayer of thanks under his breath when she declined.

At least she'd made one wise decision. He'd offered to pick her up from her community service shift, but she'd insisted on taking public transportation as if riding home with him would be a worse punishment than her court-ordered service.

She and two of her so-called friends had gotten caught with beer, setting off fireworks in the high school parking lot, one of which broke a window in the school's gymnasium. It had been a first-time offense for each of the kids, so they'd gotten off with a fine and volunteer hours.

He almost wished the juvenile court judge had imposed a stricter sentence. Maybe that would help deter Stella from further trouble.

Chase should understand. He'd been a rebellious, headstrong teenager and knew how hard it was to talk sense into someone whose frontal lobe was underdeveloped while their sense of righteous anger was blown way out of proportion.

His fingers itched to work, to make something out of the thick web of emotions inside him. For the past nine months, when everything in his life had been turned upside down, his artistic vision had gotten him through.

From the moment his estranged father and stepmother had been killed in a car crash and Chase had been named Stella's guardian, the need to create had overwhelmed him.

Emotion poured out into the blown glass sculptures he sold for obscene amounts of money in the trendy galleries that repped his work all along the West Coast. The worse his relationship with Stella became—and it had been pretty sad from the start—the more his creativity soared to new heights.

It was ironic, but he had a long enough relationship with the muse that he didn't question it.

He figured it was working for both him and his stepsister that he spent more time in the studio he'd built on his five-acre property outside the city than in the house he and Stella now shared.

He should have known better than to give a sad and angry teenage girl that much rope, enough to hang both of them.

When the kids turned the corner, Chase walked across the street, shoving his hands deep into the pockets of his wool coat. It hadn't been raining earlier, and he'd grabbed this jacket off the hook instead of something waterproof.

He knew better and smelled like a wet dog because

of it. Entering the youth center, he was immediately assaulted with the scent of apple pie.

Not what he'd expected. Nor was the woman who stood at the far end of the space wiping down the stainless-steel counter of the industrial-looking kitchen.

"I'm not interested in buying whatever you're selling." She barely spared him a glance. "If you're looking for a handout, I'm fresh out of those as well."

He was nearly rendered speechless by her brash tone and dismissive attitude. Stella had talked about Madison Maurer, the woman who managed the community center on Wednesday nights, when Stella volunteered, like she was some mix between Wonder Woman, Mother Teresa, and Betty White's ghost.

In Chase's mind, Madison had been middle-aged, probably plump since she was a chef by trade, and downright maternal. Even if, according to Stella, she cursed like a sailor when she forgot she was working with kids.

The woman ignoring him from the other side of the room was his age, maybe a year or two younger. Early thirties with wild blond hair that fell over her shoulders. She wore a vintage Ramones T-shirt and black jeans with fashionable rips at the knees. She was stunning and a complete shock to his senses.

"I'm here to talk to you if you're Ms. Maurer?"

Her hands paused in their movement, and she

gripped the sponge a little more tightly. But it took another minute for her to meet his gaze.

"Ms. Maurer was my sister before Jenna got married," she said, glaring at him. "She runs this place during the day, so you'll have to come back tomorrow."

"Madison Maurer. That's you, correct?"

She blinked and studied him more closely. "I'm Madison," she said slowly. "Do you want a gold star for getting it right?"

Chase barked out a laugh. Not at all what he'd expected. "I'm Stella Kent's…" He paused, then said, "I'm her guardian."

"The stepbrother?"

"Yes."

"You just missed her."

"I know. I'm here to talk to you. I found condoms in her bathroom, and she told me you gave them to her. She's fifteen."

"I'm aware of her age. This isn't the 1950s, Mr. Kent. We don't have to talk around protection or teenage sex."

"Call me Chase." He nodded and ran a hand through his hair. He liked it better when Madison Maurer ignored him because he was having trouble fighting the urge to fidget under her assessing blue gaze.

There was no doubt she'd judged him and found him lacking, which shouldn't come as a surprise or bother him. In this situation, it did both.

"What did she confide in you?" he asked.

She inclined her head. "She's not sexually active at this point, if that's what you're asking. But Stella needed to talk to somebody who wouldn't freak out on her. It's a mark of how desperate she feels that I was the person she chose."

"She trusts you," he said like that was some revelation. "She likes you, which is far more than she feels for me. More than she's ever felt for me, if I'm being honest."

"Have you given her a reason to feel anything else?"

"What's that supposed to mean?"

"She's a troubled girl who's been through a lot. She said you mentioned something about a convent."

"I didn't mean that, but I want to do what's best for her. Like you said, she's been through a lot. Are you telling me that you think becoming sexually active is a smart choice at her age?"

"I think what's best for Stella is to feel loved no matter what she chooses. For the record, I counseled her to wait, and I think I was convincing. But she's lost so much and feels very much alone. It's a dangerous thing for a girl to believe she has nobody. That influences how and where she chooses to find love. What she believes she deserves gets warped."

"She's not alone," Chase said.

Madison pursed her pink lips. She didn't look to be wearing a stitch of makeup but was the most beautiful woman he'd ever seen. She was clearly fierce and not afraid to speak her mind, but he could tell she truly cared about his stepsister.

Stella wasn't the only one who felt alone.

The deaths of her parents might have triggered her feelings of abandonment, but Chase's had started long before—the moment his father walked out on Chase and his mom when he was only five.

He told himself he didn't care or need anyone. That had worked for most of his life, but not since Stella had come to live with him.

Madison might not like him or approve of the way he took care of his stepsister, but she made him feel less lonely in a strange way.

"What is it that you want from me?" Madison asked.

Chase tamped down the sudden need swelling like a wave in his chest. Of all the women for his body to take notice of, why did it have to be this one?

"I want to know Stella is going to be okay."

Madison's pert nose wrinkled. "I can't promise that, but she has people here who care about her."

"I want her to know I'm one of those," he said. "She won't believe me if I tell her. Maybe she'll listen to you. I've messed up a lot but want to do better."

"Do you?"

"What's that supposed to mean?"

"Stella said something about going to live with a

friend who moved to Spokane last year. She thinks you'd prefer her out of your hair."

"No." The denial came out as a growl.

"Perhaps it's a viable option," Madison suggested, her voice quiet, "given the situation."

He couldn't decide if she believed the words or was testing him. His fists clenched at his sides. "Stella will stay with me unless I decide otherwise. I'm her legal guardian."

After a few tense seconds, Madison nodded. "You should know I gave her my number. I told her she could reach out if she needed anything. It seems important that she knows there's somebody she can trust and who's available to her."

"She can trust me."

"I believe you."

Her small concession felt like a victory.

Madison returned her attention to wiping the kitchen counter, and Chase recognized a dismissal. It had happened often enough growing up.

"Thank you. You'll never have to see me again if everything goes well."

She flashed the barest glimpse of a smile as she glanced at him through her long, spiky lashes. "Probably best for both of us."

He nodded his agreement, even though he didn't want to, and walked out into the night, heading for his truck, which was parked down the block.

Most of the Christmas lights that had sparkled

from the windows of nearby buildings when he'd arrived in the neighborhood were turned off at this point. Chase appreciated the darkness, which fit his mood perfectly.

The following week, Madison held her hands tight against her stomach as she doubled over with laughter.

"It's not funny," her friend Tessa Campbell said on a hiss of breath.

"You really are a wild child, Tess." Ella Samuelson gave Tessa's shoulder a playful shove. "I didn't think you had it in you."

"I'm married and was welcoming my husband home from a business trip."

"You were getting it on in public," Madison clarified, then laughed again.

"How were we supposed to know the Starlight bingo brigade would be on a bird-watching hike at the lake? It's normally deserted there this time of year." She pointed at Ella. "You should have warned me they had permission to access the camp property."

"Sorry, not sorry." Ella grinned. "Talk about a full moon rising. I'm surprised none of those ladies had a heart attack or fainted from the shock."

Tessa scoffed, her cheeks nearly as red as her flame-colored hair. "Trust me. They were enjoying the show."

"Gives new meaning to the idea of beach blanket bingo," Cory Schaeffer added, causing Ella and Madison to dissolve into giggles once more.

It had been nearly two years since Cory had moved to Starlight, Washington, with her baby and convinced—coerced and cajoled, more like it—Madison to help her host a monthly cooking club.

At the time, Cory was trying to convince her now-husband and Madison's boss at the bar where she ran the kitchen that she belonged in the tiny town nestled in the Cascade Mountains of central Washington.

Despite being overqualified to be crafting menus and cooking at a local watering hole and restaurant, Madison had been on the verge of losing her job. Not because of a lack of culinary talent, but as a result of her surly attitude. It didn't seem like she should be punished for expecting perfection. After all, she'd worked under some of the most challenging and demanding chefs in the business.

Apparently, making her staff cry on the regular was a deal-breaker for Jordan Schaeffer, the former football star who owned Trophy Room, the bar where she was still employed. Thanks to Cory.

Tessa and Ella had shown up for that first meeting, and the Chop It Like It's Hot cooking club was off to the races.

Madison had denied liking the meetings and the women for several months. She hadn't had female friends—any real friends—until that point. Her experience was with women who would backstab and sabotage instead of build each other up.

She could be ruthless and demanding and laser-focused on getting ahead. But she hadn't given much thought to the price she was paying for that.

The cost had been relationships, potential friendships and her mental and physical health.

"I'm never going to live this down," Tessa said, holding her head in her hands.

"Have another samosa," Madison urged. "Carbs make everything better."

They were meeting at Madison's house for the cooking club. She had a feeling the rest of them would have put their official connection on hold if it wasn't for the fact that, other than a few perfunctory instructions at the beginning of each session, Madison did most of the cooking.

Tonight was an Indian theme, with chicken tikka masala, samosas, saag paneer, and rice pudding for dessert. Although Madison was classically trained and had worked in some of the most lauded fine dining establishments in New York City and Seattle, she liked making food for real people.

Trophy Room was now known as much for her signature dishes as for its regional beer selection. She often experimented with her friends, who had no problem being her culinary guinea pigs.

Her phone rang where it sat on the counter, and she ignored it.

She left her sous-chef, who had her own unique ring, in charge on her nights off, so it must not be an emergency. The call flipped to voice mail and then immediately began to ring again.

"Somebody really wants to get ahold of you." Ella picked up the phone and handed it to Madison. "Have you been on the dating apps again?"

Madison took the phone and turned it to silent without looking at the screen. "I'm not on the dating apps at all. The last thing I need in my life is a man."

"Jordan hung up mistletoe above the bar," Cory warned her. "You better not get caught under it."

"No chance."

Tessa dipped her samosa in the yogurt dressing. "Can you imagine a guy trying to kiss Madison without her permission? He'd be taking his life—or at least the family jewels—into his hands."

"So funny," Madison muttered, although it was true. She hadn't been on a date in years and couldn't imagine being interested in a man.

Unbidden, a vision of Chase Kent, the annoying stepbrother of sweet Stella, popped into her brain.

She reminded herself that she would likely never see him again, which was for the best since he'd been the first man in forever to make her lady parts sit up and take notice.

The phone vibrated. "You should at least see who's calling," Ella said.

Madison checked the screen and then quickly answered. "Stella? What's going on? Are you okay?" She took a step away from the group. "Wait. Slow down. Hold tight, Stella. I'll be there as soon as I can."

Chapter Two

It was close to nine o'clock that night when Madison walked through the hospital doors at Seattle General. Immediately, Stella rose from one of the upholstered chairs in the ER waiting room and ran toward her.

Madison wasn't a hugger by nature, but what other choice did she have? She wrapped her arms around the girl's shoulders and pulled her close. "It's going to be okay," she said, having no idea whether that was true.

"They took him to surgery," Stella said against Madison's leather jacket. "The doctor came out and talked to me. He said Chase might lose part of his leg because of the way the furnace fell on it after the explosion. I didn't know what to do. There was glass and blood all over Chase. I don't know if it was in his eye or above his eye, and he was moaning, and then he stopped making noise. That was even worse because…"

"You got him to the hospital," Madison told the girl. "Calling 911 was the right thing to do."

"His studio is destroyed. Chase loves his studio. He spends all his time there. Now it's wrecked."

"He's not going to care about that. He can rebuild a studio."

"I'm sorry I bothered you, but I didn't have anyone else. Chase is proud. He doesn't have friends, but he told me he met you at the community center. I was angry, but now I'm glad. You know him, so you can help."

Madison tried to think of something comforting to say to the girl, but she and Chase hadn't exactly hit it off during their brief encounter. "I'm sure we'll hear something soon. Let's sit down."

Stella shook her head. "It's taking too long. You know people die after accidents."

Madison squeezed the girl's hand. "Chase is going to be okay," she said with more conviction than she felt. "I don't know your stepbrother well, but he seems too headstrong to let something like a little studio explosion affect him."

Just as Madison got Stella settled, the doctor came through the doors. Madison didn't care for the grim look on his face. She'd had friends who went to church every week when they were kids, and now wished she had some kind of faith to fall back on.

At that moment, her gaze caught on the plastic Christmas tree set up in one corner of the waiting room. The holiday season was the time for miracles, and although she didn't put much stock in that, she was desperate enough to wish for one of her own.

"You're with Chase Kent?"

Stella nodded. "I'm his sister."

The doctor's stern gaze flicked to Madison.

"This is my aunt," Stella said quickly. "She can hear whatever you have to say as well."

The doctor was an older man with thinning hair and a pallid complexion, so Madison hoped that meant he spent long hours saving lives and legs.

She kept her gaze firmly on the star glittering from the top of that waiting-room Christmas tree as he spoke and thanked her lucky stars for whatever nurse or administrator had set it up.

"He's going to have a long recovery," the doctor said, "but we were able to save the leg. He needs intense rehabilitation and will be wearing a patch for at least a week, but there was no damage to the cornea. Your brother is very lucky."

Stella's relief was palpable, and Madison patted the girl's shoulder.

"He's awake if you want to see him."

"I do," Stella said, then leaned into Madison more closely. "You'll come with me, right?"

"I don't think that's a good idea. You head back, and I'll finish talking with the doctor."

The doctor gestured to a young woman in scrubs who Madison hadn't previously noticed since her focus had been on the top of the Christmas tree.

"You won't leave?" Stella demanded.

Madison gave what she hoped was a reassuring smile. "I won't leave."

The girl followed the nurse as the doctor took a seat next to Madison. "Are you his wife or sister?"

"It's more of an honorary title." Madison cleared her throat. "I'm a family friend." She figured she could be forgiven for the white lie. She was desperate.

"As I said, he's going to need rehabilitation. He's lucky and somewhat…" he seemed to search for a suitable description "…ornery as well. He's insisting on not going to a rehab facility, which would be my recommendation. He wanted us to discharge him tonight, but that's not going to happen. He won't be able to drive."

"I'm sure Stella can make arrangements," Madison said, even though it sounded insensitive to her own ears.

"He'll need more care than a teenager can give. I assume as a close family friend that—"

"Oh, hell no," Madison muttered.

"Excuse me?"

"Stella and I are close," she clarified quickly. "I'm more her friend than Chase's."

"Then as her friend, can you arrange to take care of him? He's going to need a friend or family member."

Stella had just told Madison that Chase didn't have friends. Madison knew what that felt like. She owed Jenna a huge debt for coming back into her life when she had and knew that the friends she'd made in Starlight would move heaven and earth to help her. She hadn't done anything to deserve it.

She thought about Stella and Chase and what would happen if they couldn't find anyone to help. The girl was starting winter break soon. They'd talked about it last week at the youth center.

"Ma'am, I don't mean to push you into something that makes you uncomfortable, but if you can help arrange…"

"I'll make arrangements," she promised. "It's fine, Doctor. We appreciate everything you've done. I can't imagine what might have happened if Chase had been in less capable hands." She drew in a deep breath. "The two of them have been through a lot. I'll make sure they're taken care of now."

She glanced at the star again, knowing she'd need all the miracles she could get.

The past two days had been a blur, and Chase had no idea how he'd ended up blinking awake in the back seat of Madison Maurer's car, driving through the mountains of western Washington. He gazed out the window at the tall pine trees dusted with snow that flanked both sides of the highway.

If he tipped up his head, the tops of the trees gave way to a bright blue sky, a sort of gift in the northwest winter when relentless gray flooded everything. The idea for a new glass piece, a wide cylinder that would showcase blues and greens, embodying the spirit of his home state, appeared in his mind. He did his best to clear the image.

With a patch over one eye and his injured leg throbbing, who knew how long it would be before Chase could return to his studio. His sanctuary—the one place he felt at home.

He was situated behind the driver's-side seat and could see Stella smiling as she and Madison sang along to some Taylor Swift song about a red scarf.

Red.

The color of the blood that covered him after the accident. The emotion behind his anger at having been careless in the studio.

What else could have caused the explosion? In his more lucid moments, he replayed the minutes before being knocked off his feet.

Five years ago, he'd set up the studio, his dream work space, and took every safety precaution possible. He still didn't understand. The fire chief he'd met with early that morning offered little insight as they'd surveyed the wreckage. Almost as confusing and disconcerting as trying to figure out the cause of the accident was determining how Madison Maurer had become the angel caregiver who'd swept in and made arrangements for him to recover at her home in Starlight.

Her attitude remained the opposite of angelic, and he'd wanted to say no to her help. In fact, he had refused her offer, which had led to her calling him an idiot in about a half dozen different ways. Most of them would have made an angel blush, although Chase had been amused by her rant, which was something, given the pain of his injuries.

He didn't like accepting help and certainly didn't want it from this woman, who had made her opinion of him clear, but the sad truth was that he had no one else.

There were colleagues and people who worked for him in a variety of capacities, but he couldn't rely on any of them. He would have managed on his own if it weren't for Stella.

His stepsister had been unusually subdued as she sat in the corner of the hospital room, watching him while he waited for discharge orders yesterday morning. He would take Stella at full-blown snark mode any day instead of the girl with the haunted eyes who looked unprepared and somehow sadly resigned to having another family member taken from her, even one she didn't like all that much.

He couldn't allow himself to be a burden to her,

and if that meant suffering through a couple of weeks with Madison at the helm of their lives, so be it.

So he supposed he understood how he'd come to be there. What he couldn't comprehend was Madison's motivation. She volunteered with Stella, but that wasn't the same thing as becoming involved in such an enormous way.

He knew very little about the woman other than she used to be a famed chef in Seattle, and now she lived in Starlight. Chase had seen enough crash-and-burn scenarios with talented colleagues to guess what had led her to a simpler life in a small town.

At one point, he could have gone in that direction himself. Many glass artists set up studios in rural areas because of the burden on the utility grid and subsequent cost when they fired up their energy-sucking equipment.

Chase had stuck it out close to Seattle. He knew that the more recognition and fame he received, the harder it would be for his father to avoid seeing the press lauding his only son. Not that it had changed Martin's opinion of Chase or his chosen career. Chase had still hoped it rankled, although he'd come to regret his pettiness in the months after his dad's death.

"Is that the town?" Stella asked, gazing out the passenger-side window.

Chase couldn't see much from where he sat and couldn't move to give himself a better view. He hated being incapacitated in this way.

"It looks like a movie set from up here with the snow falling like it should be in a snow globe." Stella's voice was filled with wonder. She glanced into the back seat and noticed he was awake. "Chase, can you make a snow globe?"

He shook his head. "I don't do snow globes."

Stella shrugged and continued going on and on about the town.

Madison met his gaze in the rearview mirror, and one perfectly arched brow rose as if he was a massive disappointment because he couldn't or wouldn't make a snow globe to entertain his stepsister.

She truly had no idea the caliber of artist he was. Next to Dale Chihuly, Chase was the most famous glass artist in the world and had every intention of eventually eclipsing his more famous predecessor.

He cursed himself for sounding like a conceited prick as he gave her a tight smile.

He knew better than to buy into the hype that surrounded him. Reputations that took decades to build could be lost in an instant in the current art-world culture. Chase didn't have any skeletons, but he'd also never made an effort to be well-liked by his contemporaries or critics. He preferred to let the work speak for itself—only now his studio was destroyed and his body in not much better shape.

How long could he delay his current commissions? He'd been awarded a solo show at one of the industry's most prestigious galas, but he'd have to deliver seven large pieces for the installation to keep his spot.

He couldn't very well work with one functioning leg, not to mention a patch over his eye. He was not going to follow Chihuly down that road.

Rubbing a hand against his thigh and grimacing with the pain that shot into his hip, Chase tried to keep his mind focused on the present moment. There was no sense having an internal debate over his future path when he was stuck on the road to nowhere—literally.

A few days ago, his stepsister had seemed like the most significant challenge he faced. Now he would be relying on Stella and Madison when all he wanted was to be left alone to sulk and mope.

Instead, he was heading to a place that sounded like Santa's fantasy town come to life.

Chase was fresh out of Christmas spirit.

Chapter Three

It was nearly midnight when Madison walked through the door that led from her garage into the kitchen. After two days in Seattle, she'd returned home with her guests and settled Chase in the spare bedroom and Stella on the pullout in the office.

She'd defrosted a pot of chicken noodle soup and then headed for work. She'd needed to get away and hoped the time in the Trophy Room kitchen would help her make sense of the unexpected detour.

Her life had taken a strange turn. She wasn't a caregiver on a good day, let alone to a troubled teenage girl she barely knew and the man she didn't want to like.

In some ways, the job had done what she needed

it to. She'd lost herself in cooking and creating for a few hours, her emotional and physical exhaustion forgotten as she chopped, sautéed and gave instructions to her crew.

Thursday nights in Starlight meant turkey meat loaf as a special. The French chef Madison had trained under would have been horrified at how much pleasure she took in shaping ground turkey into mini loaves. She eschewed the traditional ketchup topping for a homemade tomato puree and would put her garlic mashed potatoes served on the side up against any spud recipe in the world.

Her food made people happy, and she no longer took the talent she'd been born with for granted. She also understood that an essential part of cooking was often in the details. The care and attention she took in sourcing ingredients elevated something as basic as meat loaf into a dish that people would stand in line to order.

She told her staff that she'd had family business to take care of in Seattle. To her great relief, no one questioned her, although they knew she didn't have family other than her sister, and Jenna was too rock-solid to need emergency intervention.

That was Madison's deal.

Cory had called, and Tessa and Ella texted, but she hoped she'd managed to put them off.

She needed a minute to come up with an answer to the inevitable question of why she'd inserted herself into someone else's family business when she had no place there. Unfortunately, she hadn't found that answer at the bottom of the meat loaf pan.

The physical exhaustion from a busy night in the kitchen would hopefully help her sleep tonight. Sleep had been elusive while she'd been in Seattle. She'd refused to stay at Chase's house while he was still in the hospital. It felt more intimate than she could handle.

Stella had packed a small bag, and the two of them had checked into a nearby hotel.

Madison spent most of the night listening to the rhythmic sound of the girl's breathing. She was so in over her head, which was a sensation she hadn't experienced in years. At that time, she'd had alcohol to numb her from becoming too aware of her lack of control. Now she was painfully tuned in to it.

She knew her friends would help, and she planned to talk to them tomorrow. Ella was a nurse, and she'd have ideas for Chase's rehabilitation. Tessa and Cory were both sweet and maternal, so they could give Stella the support she needed.

Madison knew she had little to contribute other than a place for the two Kents to stay.

No one could expect more of her. They were practically strangers. It wasn't as if they were going to form a meaningful bond over the holidays. She might have wished upon a star for a miracle, but even miracles had their limits.

"Why are we here?"

She startled as Chase asked the question in the darkness. She immediately hit the light switch on the wall, and Chase Kent's broad form was revealed on the couch.

"Shouldn't you be in bed? I thought the benefit of prescription drugs was you don't have an excuse not to be sleeping."

He flipped closed the laptop resting on the arm of the sofa. "I wanted to talk to you alone," he said.

"That sounds ominous, to tell you the truth. It's been a long day, a long couple of days."

He made a sound that resembled a laugh but only around the edges. "Tell me about it."

"I just got off work and smell like meat loaf." She held up the bag in her hand. "Dinner tomorrow night. I'll be working again."

She didn't typically work on Friday nights. The urge to drink had faded, but Madison didn't like hanging around a rowdy crowd.

Jordan kept things fairly tame at Trophy Room, but the holidays often saw locals back from out of town and more celebrations, which meant more drinking.

"Why are we here?" he repeated.

She busied herself with taking the containers out of the bag and placing them in the refrigerator. "I think what you mean to say is 'Thank you, Madison, for opening your home to people who need it.'"

She expected a sarcastic retort. Chase had made

it abundantly clear that he did not want to take her up on her begrudging hospitality, but he remained silent until she turned around.

He hadn't moved, but somehow the space between them shrank until she would have sworn she could feel the heat coming off him. Heat along with frustration and something she was too much of a coward to name.

"Thank you," he said quietly. "Why?"

"I don't know," she answered honestly, unable to do anything else when faced with his assessing stare. "It felt like you didn't have another option."

"That's true. But I would have worked something out. I could have hired someone or—"

"I did it for Stella," she said. "I don't know why. Your stepsister feels like she has a bond with me. Maybe I wanted to be a Good Samaritan. That's what people do around Christmas, right?"

He gestured to her home's interior, devoid of decorations other than a lopsided clay tree that Tessa's stepdaughter, Lauren, had gifted Madison. It sat on the bookshelf next to a picture of Madison and her friends at Cory's summer wedding.

She shook her head, afraid she was revealing too much. "Does it matter why?"

"I'm not used to people helping for altruistic reasons."

"You get a gold star for the big word," she said, moving toward the family room. "I'm not an altruistic person, Chase, but I'm helping. And you're here, which means you've accepted it. Let's make the most of it for Stella."

"You care about her."

Heat rose to Madison's cheeks. In her experience, caring about someone meant being vulnerable, and being vulnerable meant being taken advantage of or hurt.

She didn't want either. "Maybe this is my good deed for the year, or I'm trying to atone for something I've done in the past."

"Atonement," he murmured. "Your turn for a gold star."

She smiled despite herself. "I'm doing this for Stella." She felt the need to remind them both.

"Thank you," he repeated. "I'll try not to get in the way. You won't even notice I'm here."

That drew a laugh from her, and she was embarrassed at the husky sound. "Promises, promises."

"I'm going to get better." He lifted a finger to the patch over his left eye.

"It's a swashbuckling look. The ladies of Starlight are going to eat it up."

He opened his mouth as if he wanted to question her. She imagined him asking her opinion of the look, and she had no idea how to answer. Her body had its own thoughts on the matter.

"Then I'll be hiding out here when I'm not going to rehab." He made a face.

"Burned by love?"

"Never came close enough to the fire to find out," he clarified.

She couldn't explain the heavy tug in her belly that resulted from those words. "Do you need help getting to the bedroom? Is everything okay?"

He gestured to the crutches leaning against the coffee table. "I'm fine."

"You will be," she assured him.

"It's funny." He placed the laptop on the coffee table. "When I try to convince myself, it sounds ridiculous, but when you say it, I believe you."

"Maybe I missed my calling. Should I be a life coach?"

He laughed, the sound rich like thick caramel syrup. "I'm not sure I'd go that far."

"Dr. Phil better watch his back," Madison said with a smile. "I might be coming for him."

"I appreciate you taking care of Stella and me on your way there."

"You're going to be okay."

He closed his eyes, and she knew he was thinking about Stella. "I still can't believe my dad would trust me with her. It shows you how much faith he had in his own immortality. There's no way he would have made me Stella's guardian if he had any clue I would have to step up in that role."

"I don't think you give yourself enough credit."

He put a hand on his leg. "I nearly blew myself to

bits after my stepsister could have been sent to juvie for starting a fire in the high school gymnasium."

"She never mentioned why she got into trouble." Madison sniffed. "If it makes you feel any better, I did worse things when I was her age and later."

"Should that make me feel better? You turned out okay."

She shook her head. "My lowest point was nearly six months spent starting the day with a swig of vodka and finishing it at the bottom of the bottle. I sacrificed way too much on the road to recovery. You do not want her to turn out like me."

"I didn't know Stella's mother well. She was about fifteen years younger than my dad and thought the sun and moon rose by him. I don't know where that left my stepsister. Until six months ago, I didn't care. You care, Madison."

"But I don't want to," she admitted.

"Then we make quite a pair."

Didn't the thought of that take her breath away?

"I'm going to call my friend who's a nurse in the morning. She's not working in that capacity now, but she grew up in this town. She'll help get you into a good physical therapist."

The warmth she'd seen in his eyes disappeared, and she told herself it shouldn't matter. It was better they remember who they were to each other—people who had a troubled girl in common but nothing more.

She couldn't allow it to be anything more.

"You need a Christmas tree," he said as she started to back away.

"I didn't see any decorations in your house."

He nodded. "Yeah, but Stella made me promise I would at least get a tree."

"I'll consider a tree," Madison told him. It felt like a small concession. "Although I'm not much for Christmas spirit."

"That makes two of us."

Once again, she wasn't sure how to feel about having something in common with Chase.

He cleared his throat. "I have more work to do—meetings and deadlines to reschedule. I can make it back to the bedroom."

"I'll see you tomorrow."

"I'll be here." He laughed without humor. "It's not like I can go anywhere else."

"Good night, Chase."

"Good night, Madison," he answered.

The words felt close to a caress, and she hurried to her bedroom before her knees started to melt.

Chapter Four

By the time Chase's first physical therapy appointment ended, he was dripping with sweat, and the muscles in his leg burned like someone was prodding them with a branding iron. The physical therapist, who'd appeared compassionate when they first met, now seemed more like a sweet sadist, intent on pushing him to his physical limit.

That was bad enough, but he hadn't expected to also be pushed mentally and emotionally. He didn't like weakness and relied on his strength and independence to see him through any struggle.

Maneuvering out of the medical center on his crutches, he felt as helpless as a baby. He'd insisted on crutches and not a wheelchair, even though his doctor and now the physical therapist had recommended a wheelchair, given the extent of damage to his left leg.

Chase didn't want to rely on another person for basic mobility. He'd learned a couple of hard lessons about what happened when he let other people take care of him. It never worked out well. He wasn't about to give it a chance now.

Stella was sitting on a bench near the front door, her arms pulled tight around her as if to ward off the cold.

"Why aren't you waiting in the lobby?" he demanded. "The temperature is freezing, and it looks like snow. We've talked about needing a coat. You're going to catch a cold."

She rolled her eyes. "What is it with you and your obsession with jackets? I'm wearing a sweatshirt. It's fine."

"It's not fine. It's a shirt."

"A sweatshirt."

"You're supposed to wear a jacket over it. Why do teenagers have such a deep distaste for outerwear these days?"

She pointed to the beanie perched at a jaunty angle on her head. "I have a hat on, which should make you happy." She held up a hand when he would have answered. "Never mind. Nothing makes you happy."

He shook his head. "Plenty of things make me happy."

"Name one."

"Being able to craft the perfect glass bubble," he answered, and suddenly the skin under his eye patch began to itch like microscopic bugs were crawling across his face. He couldn't even scratch it because he might topple over if he released the death grip he had on his crutches.

The damage to his eye would heal, but who knew if he'd ever be able to return to his craft at the same level? Who was Chase without his work? The nobody his dad had always accused him of being.

"You sure don't look happy now," Stella murmured, stepping away from him.

Chase heard something under her teenage attitude that sounded like actual concern.

"I'm not happy with the current situation, as I'm sure you can appreciate." He took a seat on the bench next to her. "I still don't understand how the accident happened. I'm careful with my equipment. Every time, I check the blowpipe for debris and make sure all my tools and supplies are set up correctly."

He wasn't going to get answers so far away from his studio, but he reminded himself that his pain was a drop in the bucket compared to the emotional trauma Stella had been through after losing both of her parents. She might not like Chase very much, but they both knew he was all she had right now.

The truth was he'd been damn lucky not to lose more than a chunk of flesh. His injuries were nothing compared to what could have happened in an explosion like the one that had started the fire in his studio.

"I lost count of the people who told me accidents are a part of a bigger plan," Stella said, her tone sharp with anger. "I should find blessings in loss and hope in the hardship." She sniffed. "Sometimes bad things just show you that life sucks."

"You shouldn't say 'sucks,'" Chase told her as emotion balled in his chest and threatened to crawl up his throat. He didn't want to feel that emotion, so he ignored her pain and focused on the one sliver of normalcy he could respond to.

"I'm fifteen," she reminded him. "I can say…" She let out a sound of disgust. "What do you care how I talk?"

"I don't," he lied. "But your parents probably would. Dad never liked swearing. He said it made people sound cheap. I can't imagine he changed that much." Their father had been a plumber, proudly blue-collar, and not interested in having an artist for a son.

His stepsister blinked. "He said he might not have a college education, but he would talk with class."

"Sounds like Dad." Chase leaned his shoulder against hers for a brief moment. "I'm not in the market for blessings or hope. Answers, maybe, but that will have to wait. I'm fine, Stella. Physical therapy is showing me I have a long way to go in my recovery. As you might have realized, I'm not exactly a fan of being patient. It isn't one of my stronger virtues."

"I didn't realize you had any virtues," she countered, and he smiled because the anger was gone from her voice. He'd take her teasing over sorrow anytime.

Chase's father had raised Stella from the time she was a baby after Martin Kent married Stella's mother. She might not be Martin's biological daughter, but there were moments when she could offer a retort so much like one he'd expect to hear from his dad that it nearly stole his breath.

The ironic part was he admired her most in those moments. She'd clearly had a great relationship with Chase's father and seemed devastated by his loss. In Chase's experience, Martin was not an easy man to love, so he knew the teenager shivering next to him was resilient.

"Obviously, my merits can't hold a candle to yours. You must have made quite an impression on Madison Maurer. There's literally no one in my life who would have stepped in the way she has."

Madison had not only offered to have them stay with her over winter break but arranged for his follow-up care with a local orthopedic surgeon and rehab at a physical therapy clinic in the quaint mountain town. Chase would have just paid somebody to take care of things, but his sister had wanted to go to Starlight.

He guessed her motivation had something to do with finishing the final week of the semester's classes online before break started, but he'd been too weak and exhausted to argue. Now his attempt at a compliment seemed to embarrass Stella.

"It's not a big deal," she muttered.

It was a big deal to Chase, even though he was still surprised that he'd allowed himself to take Madison up on her offer.

Before he could answer, a silver SUV he recognized as Madison's pulled into the parking lot.

"What is she doing here? I was going to use a ride-share app to call a car."

Stella gave him one of her patented shoulder shrugs. "She texted to see if we were still at the appointment and wanted lunch."

His eyes narrowed. "Madison checked in to make sure I didn't skip this appointment."

"Can you blame her?" Stella demanded. "You're so grumpy. She probably wants us out of her house."

"It's what I want, too," Chase muttered.

Stella poked his arm. "You should be nice to her."

"I *am* nice to her."

"You're not nice to anybody. That's what Dad always said."

Stella stalked toward Madison's vehicle while Chase watched, frustration and helplessness pounding through him like a drumbeat. After a moment, he slowly made his way forward.

Chase had blamed the years of estrangement from his father on his dad's initial abandonment and then years of arbitrary standards Chase could never live up to. He'd never considered the fact that someone might blame him for the animosity between them.

Had his dad truly believed Chase, who'd been a little kid when his parents divorced, at fault?

And what did it say about Chase that some dark part of him felt jealous of a girl who had been orphaned less than a year earlier?

The black cloud of his mood seemed to expand until it nearly consumed him. He was fit company for no one at the moment yet had no choice but to accept whatever assistance Madison Maurer offered.

"What does everybody think about going to get a Christmas tree?"

"A real one?" Stella asked. "I've never had a real tree. Dad didn't like how it left a mess, so we always had a fake one."

"Dad didn't like a lot of things," Chase said under his breath, but Madison ignored him. She could see the lines of tension bracketing his mouth.

She guessed physical therapy must have been a challenge, but there was also a strain between Chase and Stella that hadn't been there this morning.

She wanted to do something to defuse it, although truthfully, she didn't like the thought of pine needles shedding all over her house any more than their late father did. She'd heard a couple of the kids at the community center in Seattle talking about having real trees at their homes, and she'd seen the wistfulness in Stella's gaze, so she figured that would be something the girl might enjoy since Chase had promised her a tree.

"We can go later if you need a rest," she told Chase when she noticed him massage a hand over his thigh.

"What I need is a drink."

"Then you'll need a trip into town because there's no alcohol at my house."

"Can we go now, Chase?" Stella asked. "We can drop you off at a bar while Madison and I get the tree."

Chase blew out a laugh. "I was making a joke. Sort of."

"It's fine if you can't handle it," Stella said in the way of clueless teenagers.

"I can drop you off at home," Madison offered, now wishing she'd paid more attention to his level of fatigue before she'd made the suggestion. "It's not a big deal."

"Just to be clear, you aren't planning to hike through the forest to Paul Bunyan the tree on your own?"

"Not one step into the woods. A new shipment just arrived to the tree lot in town," she explained. "They'll go quick. If we get one, we should do it while there's a good selection."

"Please, Chase," Stella begged. "You don't even have to get out of the car. You can nap while we find the tree."

Chase blew out a breath. "Like I'm a geriatric

grandpa instead of a man in my midthirties. Is it as bad as all that?"

Madison stifled a laugh, and Chase arched an eyebrow in her direction. "It also feels strange that you're taking so much pleasure when I have a legitimate injury."

"It probably says horrible things about me," Madison agreed with a solemn nod. Her lips were still twitching. "But I never claimed to be an angel."

For a moment, the air between them changed. An electrical charge sparked the same way it had that first night in the youth center. "Let's get a tree," he said. "I think I can manage to stay awake a few more minutes."

Stella let out a whoop of satisfaction from the back seat. "I can't wait to text Brinley. She's always bragging about how great her family's tree is. They get the biggest one they can find in the woods because they have a huge house on the water with such high ceilings."

"Seriously?" Chase turned to look over his shoulder at the girl. "There are teenage girls who brag about the size of their Christmas tree? That seems pathetic."

"She brags about everything," Stella said, sounding annoyed. "When we were in third grade, her mom and mine volunteered together at the school, even though my mom didn't have much time because she worked. Brinley would get mad because teachers liked my mom better than hers. Now she and her mom don't have any competition, and they can act fake nice because I'm so pitiful."

Madison squeezed shut her eyes for a moment and felt her grip tighten on the steering wheel. She didn't know what it was like to have a mom who would show her face at the school for anything but a mandatory meeting with the principal when her daughter got into trouble. Yet she understood pity from other kids and how that kind of judgment could eat away at a young soul.

"Maybe you're misinterpreting this friend of yours," Chase said, none too helpfully, as far as Madison was concerned. "You've been through a lot. You might be overly sensitive."

"Who wants to listen to holiday songs?" Madison asked cheerfully. Madison didn't usually do cheerful, so her voice sounded squeaky to her own ears, but she was going for it. "Classics or updated pop versions?"

"How would you know?" Stella demanded of her brother. "You don't know anything about my life. You haven't come to one activity at the school."

"I came to the principal's office when you and your friends shot a firework through the gymnasium window."

Madison fiddled with the button on the radio. "What do you guys think? Is Mariah Carey deserving of all her Christmas accolades? Has anybody played Whamageddon?"

Stella leaned forward, distracted for the moment, just as Madison had hoped. "What is Whamageddon?"

Madison hid her smile. "It's when you try to avoid hearing the song 'Last Christmas,'" she explained. "Personally, I don't mind it. I'm an old-school George Michael fan."

Chase gave her a look like she was speaking another language, then turned his attention back to Stella. "I didn't think you wanted me there. You never asked me to come."

Would the man ever stop shoving his foot in his mouth?

"I never asked Mom and Dad to come, either. They did it because it's what parents do. I know you're not my parent, and you're stuck with me. Now you're stuck in Starlight, and it's all my fault."

They'd made it into town, and Madison parked near the Christmas tree lot in an open space.

"What do you mean it's all your fault?" Chase unbuckled his seat belt and turned to face his stepsister. "Your parents' accident was not your fault. A drunk driver swerved across two highway lanes to hit their car." A muscle ticked in his jaw. "You need to understand it wasn't your fault."

"They were on the way home from my school play. If I hadn't gone to a cast party, maybe they would have taken me to dinner or we could have all been home together. They shouldn't have been on that road. I don't care what anybody tells me. There's no bigger plan."

"Is that why you quit the drama club at school? When the teacher called to ask me about it, she said you were talented."

"What does it matter?" Stella shook her head. "It's a stupid extracurricular I was doing for college. I'm not going to college."

"Of course you are."

Madison reached out to squeeze Chase's clenched hand. "This might not be the best time for that conversation. Who wants to pick out a Christmas tree?"

"I'm not going," Stella insisted. "Why do you even care? Once I'm eighteen, you can be done with me."

"I don't want to be done with you," Chase said, his voice gritty like his patience hung by a thin thread.

Madison knew the feeling.

Before Stella could respond, Madison laid on the horn. Both Chase and Stella startled and fell silent.

"Listen." Madison shifted in her seat and pointed at each of the Kents. "I'm ready to buy my first live Christmas tree, and you two are ruining the vibe with your bickering." She narrowed her gaze in Chase's direction. "It sucks."

"We're just having a conversation," Stella said from the back seat. "Also, you shouldn't say 'sucks.'"

"Yeah," Chase agreed and nodded. "It's a tree. Not a big deal."

Okay, Madison could appreciate that the two of

them were finding some common ground, even if it meant they were ganging up against her. But she still wouldn't let them get away with destroying this moment.

"You aren't fooling me." She crossed her arms over her chest. "Choosing a Christmas tree means something to each of us, and maybe we don't like admitting we have feelings. I sure don't like it. I'm a damn pro at repressing my emotions and using deflection as a weapon. I almost lost my job here in Starlight because of it a while back."

She straightened her shoulders. "But I'm working on it, and you both are going to as well. We're embracing some damn holiday spirit. All of us."

"Wow," Stella murmured. "I'm catching all the feels right now."

"Glad to hear it." Madison grabbed her purse from behind the driver's seat. "Also, there's a jacket in the back you can put on so you don't catch your death of cold."

"Oh. My. God." Stella gave a sigh for the ages. "You are both the same." With a great deal of fanfare, she exited the SUV, slamming the door with impressive force.

"We're not the same," Madison said, suddenly feeling self-conscious about what her rant might have revealed. "At all."

Chase nodded. "At least we can agree on that."

She opened her door to get out, but his hand on her elbow stopped her. She looked over her shoulder.

"Thank you again." He flashed a grin so unexpected it made her stomach explode with butterflies.

Silly stomach.

"Both for the jacket comment and, more importantly, for stopping the argument."

"It's not over," she told him. "You and Stella have a lot to work out."

"Yeah." He ran a hand through his thick hair, one errant lock curling over his forehead. Madison was far too tempted to smooth it away. "I get that. But I'm going to kick your butt at Whamageddon. I don't ever listen to holiday music."

"Welcome to Starlight, buddy. There aren't enough earplugs in the world for you to avoid Christmas songs in this town. It's only a matter of time."

He laughed softly, and she was glad she'd been able to make things a little better for him. Madison might not understand why it mattered any more than Chase did, but she was determined to help him and Stella heal their relationship.

Maybe she saw too much of herself in the girl. What would have become of her if she'd had someone to step in when her life went off the rails?

She'd been sixteen and living on the streets, trying to survive while missing her younger sister and grieving their mom's death. She knew Chase wouldn't allow anything dire to happen to Stella, but Madison also understood how willful a teenage girl could be.

She grabbed the crutches from the back of the SUV and brought them to Chase. Stella had walked over to the tree lot and turned to wave to the two of them.

"I found it," the girl called. "The perfect tree. It's here."

"We'll be right over," Madison answered with a smile.

"What just happened?" Chase asked, his voice suspicious. "She was ready to kill me when she got out of the car. It hasn't even been five minutes, and she's smiling again. She looks happy. What's going on?"

"She found the tree she wants. Don't you remember being a teenager and how your mood could change on a dime?"

He shook his head. "I mostly remember being angry at my dad for leaving and starting over with a new family. *Happy* wasn't part of my equation."

"Relatable," Madison conceded. "Lucky for you, Stella isn't quite as grumpy. My advice is to take advantage of it. Plaster a big smile on your face and let's pick out a tree."

She glanced at his leg. He balanced on the crutches, but she could still see remnants of pain in the faint lines fanning out from his eyes. "Are you sure you're good?"

"I'm nowhere near good, but I refuse to wait in the car like an invalid."

"No one thinks that."

"I look like a pirate with a bum leg."

She inclined her head and pretended to study him. "We could get you a pretend peg leg to sell the concept."

"Is that your idea of making me feel better?"

"Go catch up with Stella." Madison pointed toward the food truck parked to one side of the tree lot. "My idea of making you feel better is hot chocolate with whipped cream."

When he raised a brow, she rolled her eyes. "Not spiked."

"I wasn't thinking of alcohol." His smile had turned devilish. "I was contemplating all of the creative uses we might find for the whipped cream."

She gaped even as a cascade of longing rushed through her. "You can't say that to me. How did your mind immediately go there?"

"Apparently, Stella isn't the only one who can change on a dime," he said with a laugh, then headed toward the tree lot.

Chapter Five

Chase was still laughing as he approached his stepsister. Of course, he hadn't been serious with his comment to Madison.

He understood and respected the parameters of their relationship. Even though he didn't like needing help, he appreciated her giving it to him. Chase wouldn't do anything to jeopardize that or Stella's happiness.

Any man in his right mind would entertain those sort of thoughts when it came to Madison. Her brash confidence was sexy, although the glimpses of her softer side made her even more appealing to Chase.

But now wasn't the time to dwell on inappropriate thoughts about the woman who was, for all intents and purposes, rescuing Stella and him. He couldn't imagine it would ever be the right time. His thoughts immediately returned to the present as he noticed the teenage boy standing next to Stella.

"Hey there, Stel," Chase said as he got closer. "Where's this amazing tree, and who's your new friend?"

Stella let out a long-suffering sigh. "He's not my friend. I don't have friends in Starlight."

"I could be your friend," the boy said. He was tall and gangly with floppy blond hair and the tiniest bit of scruff on his chin. He shoved a hand toward Chase. "Hello, sir. My name is Brody Goodwin. I was telling your daughter—"

"My *sister*," Chase said on a choked breath. "Do I look old enough to have a teenage daughter?"

"Don't answer that." Stella shifted toward Brody. "It's a trick question."

The kid nodded solemnly. "What did you do to your leg, sir?"

"I injured it kicking the butt of the last kid who sniffed around my sister."

"You are so embarrassing," Stella ground out, and even Chase admitted he was being a little heavy-handed with the protectiveness.

It was just that the group of boys Stella hung around in Seattle had led her into trouble with the al-cohol and fireworks. He didn't know one thing about

Brody Goodwin, but he knew for sure he wanted Stella to stay out of trouble.

"I work here," Brody said, as if that explained everything. Which it sort of did. "I'll be tying up your tree and helping load it onto your car."

Chase needed to lighten up but wasn't sure how to manage it at this point. "How old are you, Brody?"

"Almost sixteen, sir."

"Does your family run the tree lot?"

Brody nodded. "My uncle. The trees come from a farm in Oregon. Stella mentioned that you were worried about shedding, but our trees have excellent needle retention."

Chase looked between the two teenagers. "You were talking about trees?"

A deep voice bellowed Brody's name from the other side of the lot. The kid held up a finger. "I'll be back in a minute."

"Seriously, Chase." Stella gave him a disgusted look. "Did you think I was planning to sneak out to party with the Christmas tree boy? I made a mistake back in Seattle. Have you never made mistakes?"

"I've made plenty," he answered without hesitation. "That's why I worry. I want something better for you. You've been through a lot and—"

"You don't trust me."

"I don't trust teenage boys."

"Who wants hot chocolate?" Madison asked as she joined them amid the Christmas trees. The smell of the drink drifted toward him, mixing with the pine perfume into an appealing, festive scent that seemed to epitomize the holiday season.

Chase felt a modicum of his irritation diminish as he took the drink from her. Stella sipped and kept her gaze on the ground.

"What happened now?" Madison demanded. "I thought we were getting the perfect tree. Did someone rush in and haul it off? I'm not afraid to go Grinch on the good people of Starlight." She reached out and tugged on one of Stella's thick braids. "Stella Lou Who here should have the tree of her dreams."

Stella's expression gentled, and she smiled at Madison. Once again, Chase appreciated Madison's gift for connecting with the girl.

"Chase thought I was trying to get with some boy I just met."

Madison gave him an arch look, communicating without words that she thought he was the world's biggest idiot, which was exactly how he felt.

"It isn't Stella I mistrust. It's the boy. I used to be a teenage boy, you know."

"Apparently, you still have the maturity of one," Madison told him. "Enjoy your hot cocoa," she said to Stella before turning again to Chase. "And the whipped cream."

Even though Chase was frustrated beyond belief, he felt his lips twitch at her teasing tone. She really was something special…someone who fascinated him, if he were being honest.

"Is Brody the boy in question?" she asked.

Stella nodded as she drank her hot chocolate. Chase noticed twin spots of color blooming on her cheeks.

"I know his family. He's a good kid."

"He seemed nice." Stella gave another heavy sigh. "I talked to him for like five minutes. How am I supposed to make friends if Chase *chases* them all away?"

"Do you want to make friends while we're here?" Chase studied his sister as she studied her drink. He suddenly realized how strange it was that Stella wanted to spend the whole winter break in Starlight. He didn't have a lot of experience with teenagers— any before Stella—but she always seemed to be FaceTiming or texting with friends.

Why had she agreed to uproot herself without a fight?

"I don't care either way," she said. "I'm sure people around here already have friends."

"It's a welcoming community," Madison said. "Or so I've been told. This might come as a surprise, but I'm not much of a social butterfly."

It was Stella's turn to choke back a laugh. "Really? I wouldn't have guessed that about you."

"Let's see this tree," Chase said when Madison's smile made his heart beat double-time. He glanced at the tall Douglas fir behind his stepsister with its broad branches and surplus of needles. "It's big, but I think—"

"That's not it." Stella led them around the corner to where the scraggliest Christmas tree Chase had ever seen sat in a lonely corner. "This is the one I want."

"It's got a bit of a hole," Madison observed, her voice not revealing her thoughts. "The branches aren't quite as full as with some of the others."

"It needs a home," Stella told them.

Chase grinned at his sister. "You picked a Charlie Brown Christmas tree."

"I don't know what that means."

"Come on. The television show with the Charlie Brown Christmas tree?"

"I know who Charlie Brown is." Stella made a face. "I've seen his dog. Snoopy, right? But I never watched a show about him."

Madison smiled. "I know what we're renting tonight. Are you sure this is the tree you want? It's not exactly one you're going to brag about on social media."

"We can make it into something special. We can give it a home."

Chase didn't like the way his chest pulled tight at her words. "It's a Christmas tree, not a pet."

"And the one I want," Stella insisted just as Brody reappeared at the end of the aisle.

"Hey, did you decide on Herman? Great choice."

Chase glanced at Madison. "Did he just call that tree Herman?"

"I did." Brody ruffled his shaggy hair with a gloved hand. "I got in the habit of naming the trees. Not all of them but the ones that seem special."

"This one is special," Stella murmured.

"Herman's my favorite, and he barely sheds. I know he doesn't look like much, but he's a good tree. He's going to make the holiday outstanding for you guys."

Madison laughed softly. "This is not how I expected buying a tree to go."

"Another thing we have in common," Chase told her. The good news was he trusted Brody Goodwin a lot more than he did a few minutes earlier. The thought of a teenager who named trees was about as threatening as the Lorax showing an interest in his stepsister. "Brody, will you help us get Herman ready to go?"

"You bet." The boy pulled a tag from the tree. "He's marked down, too. You can take that to my uncle at the register. He'll ring you up, and I'll carry out Herman."

"I can help," Stella offered.

Before Chase could tell her no, Madison grabbed his hand. "Let's go check out."

He was so disconcerted by the feel of her soft fingers enveloping his that he followed without argument.

"I think it's cute she met a boy. You're only here for a couple of weeks, which makes it even better. She can have an innocent holiday crush before she returns to her life in Seattle."

Chase growled but didn't argue. "I have no idea what I'm doing with her."

"No one would guess that," Madison said, and he squeezed her fingers.

"You're a regular comedian. I thought she had friends in Seattle, but now I'm questioning everything. Shouldn't she seem more upset about being away from home?"

"I think you gave her quite a scare," Madison answered. "I have a feeling she's just relieved that you're okay."

He wasn't okay. Or anywhere near okay, but he wasn't about to admit it to Madison, Stella or even himself.

Two afternoons later, Madison was alone in the Trophy Room kitchen when Cory Schaeffer walked in.

"Both Sophie and Miles called in sick this morning," she told her friend, "so unless you're ready to chop vegetables for the chicken potpie special tonight, I don't have time for idle chitchat."

"Where's a white flag when I need it?" Cory asked with a gentle smile. "I'm here to help."

Madison pointed a spatula in her friend's direction. "Did your husband call you?" Jordan meant well, but he was too kind for his own good. "Because that guy needs to mind his own business. I've got it under control."

"Are you sure?"

Madison looked around the kitchen that had become her home away from home and threw up her arms. "Of course. I'm here alone, the way things always end up for me."

"Not always." Cory pointed to herself. "I'm here now. What do you want me to do?"

"Not cut off your finger, for one thing," Madison answered as Cory grabbed a huge knife. Madison gingerly took that one from her and handed her a smaller chopping blade. "Start with the carrots. If you're going to lecture me, you might as well make yourself useful while you're doing it."

"I prefer to think of it as a conversation."

"I'm fine."

"That's not what I hear. What's going on? Is it the holidays? This can be a rough time for people."

"Not for you." Madison stirred the pot of cream sauce simmering on the stove. "You have the perfect husband and a perfect baby, and you probably have loads of Christmas decorations in your house."

"A few," Cory admitted with a smile. "You know that wasn't always the case for me. I've never seen this time of year bother you."

Madison sniffed. "I couldn't care less about the

holidays." That wasn't exactly true, but she usually pretended all the festive togetherness didn't affect her. "I don't even notice other than the annoying music and gaudy lights. But one of my holiday house-guests is even Grinchier than me. Chase's mood is affecting Stella's mood. I'm not exactly known as a ray of sunshine, so I don't know what to do to make things better for them."

"It's not your responsibility to make things better. You invited two people you barely know into your home."

"Chase, yes, but I know Stella. I used to be her. Well, a version of her. I want to make sure she doesn't completely turn into me."

"There's nothing wrong with you."

"We both know that isn't true. You wouldn't be here if there were nothing wrong with me. I'm chasing away my staff. Again. I thought I'd learned how to treat people, but I've been insufferable lately. I want to help this girl."

She blew out a breath. "And Chase, but he barely comes out of his room other than going to physical therapy. I bought a Christmas tree, Cory. I don't do Christmas trees, and now I have this pathetic, naked tree representing my latest failure."

"Have you decorated it?"

Madison tasted the sauce, and the creamy goodness exploded on her tongue. At least she could still successfully manage one aspect of her life. "I'm not doing it by myself, and neither of them will help. It's not even a cute tree."

"Most Christmas trees look better with decorations. Some twinkle lights and cheery red balls. Did you get ornaments?"

Madison scowled. "Of course. They're in bags in the back of my car."

"I can't believe you haven't had a tree before now."

"This is why it was a terrible idea for me to intervene. What do I know about Christmas and celebrating and being happy?"

"You know about being happy."

"I don't know how to make other people happy." She waved a hand at the empty kitchen. "I think my staff calling in sick today is proof. Maybe Jordan should have fired me back in the day. You were around to help soften my edges. Now you're not. Tessa and Ella have their own lives and important stuff going on."

She was surprised at the ache in her heart as she thought about the friends she'd made and how she feared they were leaving her behind. "You know, we didn't even meet last month for cooking club. We always meet, but you three don't need it the way I do anymore."

"Sweetie ..." Cory took a step forward.

"You aren't going to hug me," Madison said. "Not with a knife in your hand."

"Do you think I'm going to stab you?"

"I think I don't trust you enough to handle both correctly. It's fine. I don't want a hug."

Cory placed the knife on the stainless-steel counter. "Please put down the wooden spoon, because I'm afraid that if I reach for you, you'll smack me with it. For the record, I may seem gentle, but I'm scrappy in a fight."

Madison chuckled despite herself. "I'm being ridiculous."

"I'm sorry if you feel like we're not making time for our friendship. You're important, Madison."

"It's not a big deal. I don't even know why I said it."

"I'm glad you did. Keeping emotions bottled up only lets them fester. I have a feeling that's what your two houseguests are experiencing. It sounds like they've been through a lot. He could have hired a nurse. He has plenty of money, right?"

Madison nodded. "He's famous in the art world. Why did I insert myself into their lives, and why did he let me?"

"Because you needed to do it, and despite everything, Chase wants your help. He needs it. You can't come this far only to give up with a naked Christmas tree in your family room."

"The tree's name is Herman," Madison told her friend.

"The tree has a name. I like it."

Madison appreciated that Cory didn't poke fun

about Herman. "Maybe they should stay with you instead? You have all the Christmas stuff down to a science. Or I could ask Tessa. Most people don't even like me."

Cory shook her head. "I'm sure Chase and Stella like you. They aren't—"

The swinging door that led to the main bar opened, and Miles entered the kitchen.

"I thought you were sick," Madison said. "Shouldn't you be at home in bed binge-watching bad TV?"

Miles shook his head. "I'm not sick."

Madison glanced between Cory and Miles when they shared a look. "What's going on? You know I don't like surprises."

Cory fought a grin. "We hope this will be an exception."

Sophie appeared next, along with Jordan.

"Is this an intervention?" Madison demanded. She turned down the flame on the stove because she didn't want the sauce to burn and couldn't trust herself to keep watch with panic crawling through her. "I know I've been hard to deal with the past couple of days. I'll do better."

Jordan walked forward and put a red knob in her hand. "Merry Christmas, Madison. I wanted to wait until closer to the holiday, but these two—" he hitched a thumb at Sophie and Miles, who were now grinning wildly "—they didn't think they could keep a secret from you for that long."

"What?" She stared at the knob.

"It's for the new stove." Sophie clapped her hands together. "Your dream stove. It's being delivered today."

Madison's panic transformed into tingling exhilaration. "I don't understand." She met Jordan's amused gaze. "You said it was too expensive."

He shrugged. "Your two dedicated minions convinced me it was essential." He glanced past her toward the ancient gas range original to the kitchen. "I didn't realize only two of the burners on that old thing still work."

"We manage," Madison muttered. "I don't understand. I called the manufacturer. They told me the model I wanted was on back order for over a year."

Sophie took a step in her direction. "You can thank Miles for that. He called the corporate office in Wisconsin every week because they told him if they got an order cancellation, we might be able to jump ahead in line if we paid cash."

"I called and Sophie emailed," Miles said, placing an arm around the sous-chef's shoulders. "We knew how much it meant to you, and we wanted to get it here for Christmas."

Madison blinked. "Why?"

"Because we thought it would make you happy."

"But I've been awful lately."

Miles chuckled. "Everyone has a bad day, Chef.

Maybe you have a few more than most, but you don't give yourself enough credit."

"We know what you did for us, Chef." Sophie breathed out a long sigh as she leaned against Miles's shoulder. "You paid for rehab for my brother."

"And took care of my mom's medical bills after her fall."

Madison felt her face grow hot. "I did those things anonymously, not because I expected payback. How did you even find out?" She turned to Jordan, who held up his hands, palms out.

"It wasn't me. And they handled the whole thing. I just wrote the check."

"A bigger check than the bar can afford," Madison told him.

"I can afford it," he countered.

"I don't know what to say," Madison whispered.

"Thank you?" Cory suggested under her breath.

"Right. Thank you." Madison came forward and gave her two staff members a stiff hug, making them both laugh. She was a notoriously lousy hugger. "This is beyond what I could have imagined."

"You're a good boss," Sophie said.

Miles nodded. "A good person, even though you don't like people to know it. We appreciate you, Chef."

"I thought you were both going to quit," Madison said with a bewildered smile. "I figured I was chasing you away. I'm glad that's not the case, and I'll try to be less...well, like me."

Miles winked as she pulled away. "All of the work of getting this thing here was worth it just to experience Madison Maurer trying to give somebody a decent hug."

"I'm a great hugger." Madison swatted the young man on the shoulder. "It's rude of you to suggest anything else. I'll forgive your insolence because of the dream range you procured for me."

Sophie leaned in. "You take care of people. We know it's not just us. There's talk of a guardian angel in town who swoops in to help families in need. It seems like a strange coincidence that most of the families in question include people who are regulars at Trophy Room."

"That's a definite coincidence." Madison crossed her arms over her chest. "But it doesn't explain why the two of you flaked on me this morning. You know chicken potpie night is popular." She wanted the attention off herself.

At that moment, an older gentleman with a bushy beard and very little hair on top of his head came through the door. "Is this where I'm setting up the range?" He glanced around the kitchen. "The boss said I gotta get it off the truck today so he gets some peace and quiet."

"We might have had to do a little personal persuading to get the range here promptly," Sophie said in a conspiratorial whisper.

Madison swallowed down the emotion clogging

her throat as Jordan nodded at the delivery guy. "You can pull around to the alley in back, and we'll bring it through the double doors. Appreciate you delivering it."

"You bet," the man answered with a nod of his own. "Want me to haul away the old one?"

"We've got no use for it," Jordan said.

Madison held up a hand. "Actually, if you could leave it in the alley, I've got someone who will pick it up. It's in good enough working order for my sister's youth center." The delivery guy nodded again and exited the room.

Afraid her expression would reveal how deeply moved she was by the gesture, Madison turned her back on her two employees and Cory and Jordan. "I just need to get the pots off and—"

"We'll take care of everything," Sophie told her. "You go get lunch with Cory or something."

Madison sniffed. "I can help."

"We want to do a big reveal," Miles explained. "See if we can get you to cry. That might be even more awkward than the hug."

"It's a good thing I'm so excited about my new stove," Madison told him, regaining enough composure for a pointed glare. "Otherwise, you'd be in big trouble with that attitude, buster."

The twentysomething's grin widened, and Sophie gave her a little push toward the swinging door. "Don't worry," she said before Madison could protest. "While he's installing it, I'll get caught up on the vegetables. We'll make sure the potpies are ready to go before tonight."

Madison followed her friend into the front of the bar, still dazed by the effort her two staff members had gone to on her behalf. It was quiet, the winter sun shining into the empty space.

In a couple of hours, the bar would fill with regulars who came as much for her food as for a drink and the camaraderie.

"Do we need to debate whether you make people happy again?" Cory asked, cutting into Madison's musings. "I think Sophie and Miles answered that question for you."

"They didn't have to go to the trouble. Jordan didn't have to make that kind of investment."

"They wanted to, and so did he," Cory told her. "Not that I'm totally surprised, but were you going to keep your guardian angel gig a secret forever? I'd been hearing murmurings throughout town for the past couple of months. I'll be honest—I didn't guess it was you."

"My money should go toward something useful. It's amazing how much extra cash I have now that I'm not spending it on booze or worse."

Cory went behind the bar to pour them each a soda. "When was the last time you had a drink?"

"Five years," Madison said without hesitation.

"Don't you think it's time to give yourself a break?"

"I hurt people. You know that."

"I know that you made mistakes."

"Mistakes that nearly cost my sister her life and robbed her of the ability to have a family of her own. I can't make that up to her, but I can try to do some good in the world."

"You told us she's forgiven you."

"I haven't forgiven myself."

"It's time."

"It's nowhere near time. Let's not talk about the past. Let's talk about my future with that sexy new range."

"Spoken like a true chef," Cory said. "There's a lesson here. Sometimes people need help, even if they can't admit it. Even if they don't know how to ask for it. Sophie and Miles didn't give up on that piece of equipment. I know it's not the same, but I don't think you should give up on Stella and Chase. You can make a difference for them, just like you want to. It may take more effort than you expected, but I think we've seen today that effort can be worth it."

Madison bit her lower lip and considered her friend's words. "Do you ever get tired of offering such wise advice?"

Cory grinned. "Not one bit."

"Okay, then." Madison took the drink Cory offered and held it up for a toast. "Operation Christmas Miracle, here we go."

Chapter Six

Chase emerged from his bedroom later that evening, drawn by the sound of music and laughter and the scent of garlic that was too delectable to resist.

He knew he was acting like a complete fool but couldn't stop himself. The doubts that plagued him about his ability to usher Stella through her last few years of childhood until she turned eighteen were a relentless pounding in his head and heart.

It had been simple enough to pretend things were okay back in Seattle. He'd even managed to chalk up her behavior to normal adjustment pains after a loss like the one she'd suffered.

He'd let his work consume him and convinced himself that providing for her care meant nothing more than food, shelter and clothing. A few days in Starlight had shown without a doubt that his plan of living parallel lives with his stepsister was not going to cut it. He was also disconcerted by how much he missed his art but not the rest of his solitary life.

With nothing to occupy his time other than physical therapy each day, he'd been left with way too many hours to ruminate over all the ways he was failing her.

And how much he hated his late father for putting him in this position.

"He lives," Madison said with a cheeky smile as he entered the kitchen. "Grab a knife and start chopping carrots."

"Why do I have to do the onions?" Stella complained, wiping the sleeve of her UCLA sweatshirt across her cheeks.

"Because teenage girls love a good cry," Madison told her.

"I came out to get a glass of water," Chase lied.

"This isn't the Ritz-Carlton." Madison pushed a cutting board with a pile of bright orange carrots on it in his direction. "Everyone pitches in to help. It's chicken potpie night at Trophy Room, so we're having the same dinner here."

Chase slowly came forward and propped his crutches against the counter. He took a seat on a nearby stool. "Shouldn't you be at work?"

"I took the night off so we could make a homemade dinner and decorate the tree."

Ah, yes. Herman. The pitiful Christmas tree had sat ignored in the front window since they'd set him up.

Chase blamed himself for that as well. He'd ignored the ache and fatigue in his leg after that first physical therapy session because he hadn't wanted to admit weakness. His body had the last laugh when they'd arrived home. He'd been helping to cut the twine that bound Herman to the top of Madison's SUV when his leg gave out completely.

He'd ended up sprawled in a heap in her driveway, doing his best not to cry out with the stabbing pain radiating through his entire body.

Stella had looked horrified, and he'd pushed Madison away when she'd tried to help him.

In his frustration, he'd muttered some choice words about wishing he could be left alone, and that was exactly what the two of them had done.

They'd stomped into the house, leaving him and the tree outside.

He'd been sulking ever since.

"Are you sure you can trust me with a knife?" he asked, touching a finger to his eye patch.

He expected some sarcastic comeback, but Madison only nodded. "I trust you."

When was the last time Chase had chopped a vegetable or made anything remotely from scratch in a kitchen? It wasn't as if he fed Stella a bunch of junk food. For years, he'd paid a service to deliver meals several times a week, but as he fell into a rhythm with the carrots, he realized that making dinner wasn't just about the food.

Stella sang along with the songs blasting from the speaker tucked under the cabinets on the counter, and Madison looked more relaxed than he'd ever seen her.

This was clearly her comfort space, the way his studio was to him. She stirred the sauce on the stove and then gave Stella a taste.

"So good," his stepsister murmured.

"The secret is in the roux," Madison explained. "Remember when we made homemade mac and cheese at the youth center? You and the other kids were so determined to get your sauce to a boil that—"

"We burned it."

"Scalded sauce is no good." Madison grabbed another spoon from a drawer and dipped it into the pot, then held it across the island toward Chase. "Patience is the key."

He imagined she was talking about more than just the food but forgot everything except the savory explosion of flavor on his tongue as he took the bite from her. He didn't know whether he derived more enjoyment from the sauce or watching Madison's delight as he groaned in pleasure.

"Your talents are wasted on bar food," he told her. The wrong thing to say once again, he realized, as she snatched away her hand.

"I'm happy in Starlight."

"Right. Sorry."

"No problem," she said, but her full lips had thinned into a strained line.

Damn. Why was he such an imbecile? Had he become so unaccustomed to having everyday conversations? In his world, Chase was king. He employed four other artists to aid him on the more significant projects but preferred to work in solitude in his home space.

Preferring not to have to talk to people.

He oversaw the installations but hadn't bothered to get to know or make an effort with the artists who worked for him or even with his clients. It was easy to fall back on the eccentric artist persona, but he was simply a jerk without that.

He didn't want to be a jerk.

"How was your day at work?" he asked Madison.

Both she and Stella paused to stare at him like he'd just asked her to dance naked around the house.

"It was incredible, actually," she answered finally. He watched her features relax, and a smile spread across her face as she dumped Stella's chopped onions into a sauté pan. "I've wanted a new range for the Trophy Room kitchen, and I thought it was on indefinite back order. My two employees worked behind the scenes to get it delivered earlier."

"Today?" he asked and pushed the cutting board of diced carrots toward her.

She added them to the pan. "Yes, and it's so beautiful. We've been getting by with decades-old equipment, but I'm slowly updating everything. I'm turning that bar kitchen into the work space of my dreams." She looked over her shoulder and arched a brow at him. "I'm happy there as well."

"Working in my studio made me happy," he offered with a shrug. "Maybe that's why I've been such a grump." He caught Stella's gaze. "Even grumpier than usual since the accident," he conceded at her pursed lips.

"It happens to all of us. At least, I can relate," Madison answered and handed his stepsister a wooden spoon. "I've turned off the heat to the sauce. Stir the vegetables until they're soft and the onions are translucent. I'm going to get the ornaments and lights from my car. We can decorate the tree while the potpie is in the oven."

"Do you need help?" Chase automatically rose from the stool, even though he wouldn't be much help on crutches.

"You keep your sister company," Madison told him. Stella looked about as excited by the prospect as Chase felt, but he nodded. He understood Madison was going way outside her comfort zone to make an effort and figured he could meet her halfway. As much as he typically wanted to be left alone, sequestering himself in the bedroom for the past couple of days hadn't been much fun.

He missed the sounds of Stella singing under her breath as she went about her day and knowing what was going on with her even if he kept himself at a distance. Was it possible to want both solitude and connection?

He wasn't sure how to make that work, but it was time to try. At least for now. "Your new friend Brody was right about Herman," he said into the silence that ensued once Madison left the kitchen. "I've been checking on him, and he doesn't seem to be losing many needles. I don't think I gave that tree enough credit."

"Just the tree?" she asked. He didn't miss the note of challenge in her voice.

"Not just the tree. I know I keep messing up with you, and you deserve better, but—"

"You're what I've got," she answered.

Not exactly warm and fuzzy. But it wasn't an outright complaint, so maybe that counted as a win.

"I'm going to work on my attitude, but I need your help. I still have no idea what I'm doing, so maybe you could clue me in every once in a while. Talk to me. Tell me what's going on at school."

"Do you even care?"

"More than I expected to."

She breathed out a soft laugh. "Points for honesty."

"I'm trying, Stella. I want to try."

She turned her back on him to fully concentrate on adding the vegetables and the pulled chicken

Madison had left on the counter into the sauce pot. When she deemed it adequately mixed, she slowly faced him.

"I want to try, too," she said, and it was like the hallelujah chorus came to life inside his heart.

Maybe he could believe in Christmas miracles after all.

"No. No way. A hundred times no. Not a snowball's chance in—"

"So you'll do it?" Madison beamed at Chase as her friends around them rolled their eyes and snickered.

Chase glanced toward Josh Johnson and Carson Campbell, who were respectively engaged and married to Madison's friends Ella and Tessa.

Tessa had invited everyone to the house on the mountain she and Carson shared for dinner. Madison had figured it would be good for Chase to interact with adults other than her and his physical therapist now that he was out of his self-imposed exile.

The previous evening had been more fun than she'd had in a long time. Not that she was turning into a full-blown fan of Christmas, but decorating the tree with Chase and Stella had softened even Madison's two-sizes-too-small heart when it came to holiday traditions.

It had to be her imagination, but it felt like Herman had perked up a bit as they'd wound colorful strands of lights around him and hung the ornaments she'd picked up at the local hardware store on his branches.

The tree had looked so fine and cheery it could no longer fit the bill on the Charlie Brown Christmas circuit. And Madison had been inspired to return to the store to purchase a few more decorations for the house and additional strands of lights to adorn her front porch.

In addition to the adults, tonight's crowd included Carson's eleven-year-old daughter, Lauren, as well as Josh's third grader, Anna.

Chase had seemed as shocked as Madison at what a natural Stella was with the little girls. She'd happily sat at the kids' table for dinner, and after enjoying the apple crisp that Madison had contributed to the meal, all three girls had gone up to Lauren's room to play dolls.

Tessa and Ella couldn't stop talking about what a sweetheart Stella was, and Madison realized she'd misjudged the girl. Based on their interactions at the youth center, Madison had assumed Stella was as much of an emotional train wreck as Madison had been.

But Stella still had an innocent heart because she'd had parents who loved her.

Madison had never felt that from a mother addicted to both men and pills. All she'd had was Jenna, and she'd almost destroyed her sister during her downward spiral.

When Tessa mentioned the youth concert at the high school she was organizing as a fundraiser for the local community center, Madison immediately suggested Stella be part of it.

The girl had a fantastic voice, and seeing her with the younger children convinced Madison it would be good for her to get involved.

Then Tessa lamented that her cochair for the event had dropped out of planning due to a family emergency. Madison thought it was a stroke of genius to volunteer Chase to step in.

He didn't agree.

"You seem like the type to wrangle kids on a Christmas cookie sugar high," Carson said with a laugh.

"Don't let him scare you," Josh advised. "I've coached Anna's soccer team for years. It's a blast."

"I also coached my daughter's soccer team," Carson added.

"You made the kids cry," Tessa reminded him.

Madison gave Chase a gentle nudge. "Don't make the kids cry."

"No chance of that." He gazed down at her, his blue gaze bright and slightly panicked. "Since I'm not volunteering." He pointed at his eye patch. "I'd probably scare the kids away."

Josh chuckled. "If you think they're going to be

put off by a patch, you really don't have much experience with kids."

"I'm taking him to the doctor tomorrow," Madison shared, ignoring Chase's glare. "No more *arrgh, matey* for this guy."

"Assuming it's healed," Chase muttered.

Madison wasn't sure what prompted her to reach out and touch his arm, but it felt right. "It's going to be fine."

Tessa held out her hand. "Give me your phone, Chase. I'll text you the practice schedule. It's only two weeks—we don't want anyone too overwhelmed leading up to Christmas, and I can pick you up if Madison isn't available to drive you."

Chase frowned. "I haven't agreed to help."

Josh handed him another beer. "But you will."

"Of course he will," Ella confirmed. "No one can say no to Tessa."

Madison could feel the tension radiating off Chase. He wasn't like Carson or Josh, who were used to being part of a group. She could tell Chase had been alone for too long, depending on only himself and not letting anyone get close.

She could relate because her life had been much the same until her friends in Starlight broke through her defenses.

But that had taken months. Chase and Stella were only staying in Starlight for a couple of weeks.

"The pageant raises money for a good cause,"

Tessa reminded them. "I don't want to take advantage of having a famous artist involved, but if you'd be willing to donate a piece for the holiday auction we're sponsoring during the reception after the concert, I'd be forever grateful." She grinned at Madison. "Madi is offering a cooking class for some lucky group."

"I am not." Madison shook her head. "I never agreed to that."

"But you will," Ella said in a singsong voice.

Chase elbowed her. "Misery loves company. If I'm getting involved, so are you."

She scoffed. "You just have to pluck some sculpture off of a shelf. A cooking class means interacting with people."

"And helping to organize an event filled with singing ankle biters doesn't?"

"You two are adorable," Ella said with a laugh. "The Christmas spirit is oozing from your pores."

Madison glanced back to see both of her friends staring at her with assessing looks. She didn't like the blush she could feel creeping up her cheeks. "Fine. I'll donate a class if Chase helps with the pageant."

"Fine," he agreed. Then his features went slack like he'd just realized what he'd agreed to.

"Told you so," Josh said under his breath.

"She'll go easy on you," Carson promised. "And I'll smuggle beer into the reception if you need it."

"I've got earplugs at the house," Josh offered.

"He won't need earplugs," Tessa countered. "It's going to be fun."

Madison bit back a smile as Chase growled low in his throat. The sound rippled across her nerve endings like a hot breeze. When was the last time she'd had this kind of reaction—any reaction—to a man? She couldn't remember ever feeling this way, which was terrifying in its own right.

Carson gestured to both Josh and Chase. "Let's go into the den and catch the last few minutes of the game."

Madison half expected Chase to argue, but he grabbed his crutches and followed Josh and Carson. He didn't seem like the type of guy to hang out, but wasn't that why she'd insisted he come along? So he could see that being an island unto himself wasn't the only option and certainly not the best one to help his relationship with Stella.

"Wow." When the three women were by themselves in the kitchen, Tessa made a show of fanning herself. "Now I understand why you insisted he come to stay with you. Dark hair. Piercing eyes. Swagger for days. Your type for sure."

"Stop," Madison told her friend. "I did it for Stella, not Chase."

"Sure, sure." Ella grabbed a can of sparkling water from the refrigerator and handed it to Madison. "Also, I eat kale salads because they taste good."

Madison rolled her eyes. "You don't eat kale."

"You get my meaning."

"They're here for the holidays, and he's recovering from a massive accident. There's nothing between us."

"Then you're a fool," Ella said matter-of-factly. "Or a bigger coward than I assumed."

"Excuse me?" Madison gaped at her friend. "I am most certainly not a coward."

Ella shrugged. "If the *bock-bock-bagock* fits, then let's call it a chicken."

Tessa stepped forward, holding an arm out to each of them. "Where is Cory when I need her to help me mediate the two of you?"

"I don't need mediating." Madison narrowed her eyes. "I'm trying to do something nice for a couple of wayward souls, and Ella wants me to turn it into a sordid booty call."

"Sordid, no." Ella shook her head. "But that guy is sexy as hell. He's got the brooding artist thing down to an art as elevated as his sculptures. And he's clearly into you."

"He can barely tolerate me." Madison crossed her arms over her chest. "The feeling is mutual."

"You like him," Tessa said quietly.

"I need new friends," Madison muttered.

"What is so wrong with connecting with a handsome man?" Ella demanded. "When was the last time you went on a date?"

Madison rolled her lips together. She hated to admit the truth out loud. "Before I stopped drinking."

Silence descended fast, and she concentrated on the pounding of her heart instead of meeting either Tessa's or Ella's gaze.

"That was five years ago," Tessa said after a moment. "You haven't…you know…"

"Been on a date or anything else since that time." Madison took a drink of sparkling water, letting the fizz wash away the sudden dryness in her mouth. "It's not a big deal. I was due for a break. Alcohol made me…" She felt the bubbles down her throat and hoped that accounted for the burning she felt. "Let's just say I wasn't exactly discriminating in my choices."

"You're different now," Tessa said, as if Madison needed the reminder. Maybe she did.

"Now you're a nun," Ella added.

Madison chuckled despite herself. "You don't understand how bad it got."

"Because you don't talk about it," Ella answered. "We're here to listen."

"Also to encourage you to remember the person you've become." Tessa patted her shoulder. "You deserve—"

"A romp in the sheets with a hot guy?" Madison rolled her eyes. "I hope that's what you were going to say, because if you start talking about love and happy endings, I will lose it. I don't want that stuff."

"I didn't, either," Ella confided. "But I'm happy I gave Josh a chance."

"Chase Kent doesn't want a chance with me." Madison hated how the words made her chest feel hollow. "He wants to recover and raise his stepsister and get back to his life in Seattle."

"Well, isn't that perfect, then?" Ella beamed. "He's like a perfect appetizer for you. No more commitment than a couple of weeks, and you're back in the saddle."

"I've never ridden a horse."

"You know what I mean. Just consider it."

Tessa nodded. "You might surprise yourself."

Madison had surprised herself on a dozen different levels lately. She was full up on surprises but could tell by the twin looks of determination on her friends' faces that they weren't going to give up.

"Fine. I'll consider a fling with Chase Kent." She closed her eyes and pictured it, her body growing heavy at the image of the two of them together. "A hot, steamy melt-my-knees connection should make up for a five-year dry spell. What's the worst thing that could happen?"

When neither of her friends answered, she dropped her arms to either side and opened her eyes.

"The worst thing?" Tessa asked in a low voice.

"Probably the fact that he's standing right behind you," Ella shared.

And Madison remembered why she'd kept to herself for so long.

Chapter Seven

Chase had heard the wood floor creak on the stairs a half hour earlier but hadn't moved.

He'd tossed and turned on the comfy mattress in Madison's guest bedroom, his gaze returning to the clock on the nightstand every few minutes like he were a kid in the last period of the day, counting the minutes until the final bell rang.

Only Chase knew relief wasn't going to come for him that easily. Not with the words he'd heard Madison speak earlier that night spinning through his head, swirling into a tornado of yearning.

He wasn't a man who yearned.

But he'd never met a woman like Madison before.

He didn't know what had possessed him to return

to the kitchen to retrieve his phone from his jacket pocket. It wasn't as if he had urgent business to attend to, but he'd had trouble allowing himself to relax with the other guys.

He'd never been great at casual conversation or normal social interactions. His dad had been a complete extrovert, a guy's guy who liked to watch sports over a beer, talking stats and playoff standings with anyone who would listen to his pontificating.

Chase had developed a rock-solid layer of armor in his quest to do the exact opposite of what his dad would want. Anger, judgment and emotional distance were the hallmarks of Chase's personality. The funny part was the surlier he got, the more the sycophants in the art world loved him.

Chase was a beast of a man who could also create delicate, dreamy art. Critics and fans devoured the dichotomy, and Chase had allowed that to be a green light for his bad temper and treatment of those around him.

But Stella didn't give a fig about his reputation or talent, and the accident clearly showed that, while the people in his world might admire his work, he didn't have friends.

There was no one he could depend on for help or support.

Other than the prickly, fickle woman he could hear down the hall who potentially wanted to have mind-blowing sex with him.

A terrible idea.

A thrilling prospect.

Chase climbed out of bed, put on a T-shirt and then grabbed his crutches from where they were propped against the wall. He hated needing them, being dependent on anything outside of himself. He had to admit that his grueling physical therapy had already made a difference. The muscles in his leg ached less, and his range of motion was improving.

Chase knew it would be easier to heal his physical wounds than the ones he'd let fester in his soul for so many years. He didn't know how to overcome those when they felt ingrained in the very fiber of his being.

As he listened to the sound of his crutches thumping along the hardwood floor, he wondered how Madison had managed not to hear his approach earlier. Had she been so wrapped up in thinking about the possibility of the two of them together that it short-circuited her brain?

Most of his thoughts had nose-dived south when she'd referred to their connection as hot and steamy. His body felt aroused even considering the possibility.

He came around the corner and into the kitchen to find her staring directly at him, hands on hips.

"No more sneaking up on me," she said in a hushed tone.

Recessed lighting turned low lit the kitchen. It gave the space a kind of cozy intimacy that seemed appropriate for the wee hours of the night. Although, it was not suitable for Chase to be thinking of Madison and the word *intimacy* in the same sentence.

"Yeah, I'm real stealthy right now." He took both crutches in one hand and hopped the last few steps to the stool at the island.

He loved her warm and inviting kitchen with stone counters and hickory cabinetry. The refrigerator was covered with the same wood panels, and the range was some vintage-looking model in a robin's-egg blue color. When he'd first met Madison in Seattle, this would have been the last type of space he'd have expected in her home.

Now he understood it fit her perfectly. She might be testy on the outside, but she cooked from the heart, and this was a space that showcased that.

"You should be asleep," she said by way of greeting.

"I could say the same about you," he answered.

"Sleep isn't my favorite pastime. My brain doesn't cooperate when it comes to shutting down."

She lowered the arm of the standing mixer and turned it on before he could speak again. They stood in silence for a minute, watching the beater twirl until she finally turned it off.

"You're a baker as well as a chef?"

One side of her mouth kicked up. "I'm not a baker. I like to bake. It's my comfort activity. I can make something easy like an apple crisp, but more complicated recipes aren't my forte."

"Is it typical that a chef isn't good at baking?"

She shrugged. "The thing that makes me good in the kitchen is my instinct for flavors. I can tell what a dish needs, and I deviate from the recipe most of the time. You can't do that in baking, so I've ended up with many pancake-flat muffins and dry cakes. More times than I care to admit."

"A culinary rebel," Chase murmured. "Why does it not surprise me that you don't love following rules?"

"I respect them," she countered, "but at this point, I understand enough to know which rules I have to follow and which ones I can ignore."

Heat flashed in her eyes, and he wondered if she was thinking about rebelling with him. It was all he could focus on at the moment.

"Your friends are nice." He moved closer. "Are you the only one that's not part of a couple?"

She blew out a breath. "It didn't start that way. In fact, they didn't start out as my friends. Tessa, Ella and Cory, my boss's wife, forced themselves on me. Now I can't imagine my life without them. But things have changed since they have... Well, yes, I'm the only one left who's single."

"Why don't you have someone in your life?"

"I failed at love."

She surprised him with her honesty.

"I failed at a lot of things, but love was one of my

more spectacular failures. Some people aren't built for deep emotions. I'm one of those."

"Me, too." He ran a hand through his hair. "I don't think I've ever been in love. I'm pretty sure I'm not capable of feeling it. In contrast, Carson and Josh seem like good guys." He felt the need to make sure she understood. "Just so we're clear, I'm not a good guy."

"Chase."

He gave a sharp shake of his head, unwilling to stop. "Which is why I've reached out to a cousin I have in Portland to see if Stella could live with her."

Madison's hands stilled on the mixing bowl. "You're going to send her away?"

"I'm going to give her an opportunity to be with someone who knows how to meet her needs and take care of her. You saw her tonight with those kids. She's got a good heart. She deserves more than I can give her."

"Is that what she wants? Have you talked to her?"

"I haven't seen or talked to my cousin Brandie since we were kids. I haven't mentioned anything to Stella, and I won't until I know it's a real possibility."

"You're going to dump her with a stranger?"

"That's exactly what my dad did to her. I was a stranger in all the ways that counted. It's been almost a year. I haven't seen her smile like she does in Starlight since she came to live with me. At first, I attributed her attitude to grief, which I understood. Then I figured she was a sullen teen. Her teachers tried to reach out, but I'm embarrassed to say I ignored them. I didn't force her into counseling. I messed up at every turn. Seeing her here, I realize Stella has a huge capacity for joy, and I'm preventing her from accessing that."

Madison took two cookie trays from a cabinet below the counter, pushed one in his direction and then handed him a metal scooper. "At least make yourself useful while spitting excuses for giving up on her."

"I would think you'd approve of the potential for Stella going to live with someone more capable and stable than me. You're so concerned about her not turning out like you."

She gave him an arch look. "I am concerned, but believe it or not, you're more stable than any situation I was put into as a teen."

He began to drop cookies onto the baking sheet, following Madison's lead. "What situations?"

"The usual clichés—a mother who prioritized booze and men over me, a string of loser boyfriends who didn't know how to keep their hands to themselves. My mom died when I was a little older than Stella. I didn't have anybody willing to take me in. They tried to put me in foster care, and I ran away. I dropped out of high school, couch surfing or sleeping on the streets until I turned eighteen. Eventually, I got a job at a restaurant and quickly worked my way up the ranks. I was good at my job, but all of those self-destructive behaviors that had become my go-to during the formative years stuck. I finally had people willing to go to bat for me, but it was too late. I couldn't get out of my own way."

"That's why I want to help Stella now. I don't want her to get to that point," he said, clearing his throat when his voice cracked. "It would be easier if I didn't care. I thought I didn't care, but I do. I know I'm not what's best for her. You have to see that, too."

He figured she'd agree straightaway, but her lips thinned. "I don't think you give yourself enough credit."

"I know who I am."

"You know the man you've been until now."

"I don't want to change."

She nodded. "You didn't think you cared, but I know what negligence looks like, Chase. My mom wouldn't have given up the last puff on a cigarette to help me. You aren't that bad, even if you want to pretend you're awful."

"Right back at you, Madison. I doubt you're trash at love," he countered. "You may not express it the way your sweet friend Tessa does, but you're some-body who has love to give."

"We're going to have to agree to disagree," she said. When the two trays were filled with neat stacks of dough, she placed them in the preheated oven.

Chase used the counter to balance as he hopped around toward her. "I've lost plenty of sleep worrying about Stella's future, but that wasn't my problem tonight."

Her breath hitched, and seemingly of their own accord, her small hands came to rest on his bare arms like she needed him to anchor her. He liked the way she felt touching him. The tiny calluses on her palms indicated she worked with her hands. He suddenly wanted to capture her spirit in a sculpture, flowing with fiery brilliance.

He'd create her in vibrant reds or deep blues and purples like the winter surf, dangerous in its beauty.

He leaned down and lightly pressed his mouth to hers, the kiss both a question and an invitation. To his surprise, her arms circled his neck, and she drew closer. Her tongue traced the seam of his lips, and he opened for her, craving the heat she offered. It felt like a fire had sparked deep within him.

In seconds, they were molded together, tongues swirling, and he caught her soft groan in his mouth. It was incendiary and more than he could have dreamed up—which was saying something, since Chase spent his life creating.

But almost as soon as things got good, Madison jerked away. Her gaze was at once hazy from desire but also sharp with frustration and, quite possibly, fury.

The contrast was pure Madison, and he didn't argue when she pointed toward the hallway. "Go," she told him, her voice trembling. "I need you to go back to your room."

With a nod of acceptance, he grabbed his crutches and retreated.

Madison turned from stirring the pot of chili on the new stove at Trophy Room the following afternoon to find Sophie and Miles staring at her.

"What? Do I have toilet paper on the back of my pants?"

"You're humming," Miles said.

"A Christmas song," Sophie clarified. "'Frosty the Snowman.'"

"Do we have some rule against humming that I don't know about?" She pointed at Miles. "You sing all the time, and your voice has all the melodic qualities of a cat with its tail slammed in a door." Her two employees grinned.

"You guys are freaking me out. What's going on?"

"Is it the new range?" Sophie asked. "Is it really that special?"

"I think it's her houseguest," Miles said. "My sister's boyfriend's cousin works at the medical center connected to the hospital. She said she's seen some superhot guy on crutches going into the physical therapy clinic. When he comes out, there's our little Madi waiting at the curb to pick him up."

"Your sister's boyfriend's whoever needs to get a hobby or pay more attention to their work." Madison made her glare as fierce as she could manage. "As do the two of you. My propensity to hum has nothing to do with Chase."

"Such a cute-guy name," Sophie said, doing a little shimmy.

"Stop wiggling your hips," Madison commanded.

"I can show you how," Sophie told her. "My boyfriend and I are taking salsa dancing classes. It's pretty sexy. It would help you to loosen up. I bet your houseguest would like that."

"Chaaasse," Miles crooned, his eyes closed dreamily before he dissolved into a fit of laughter.

"You two are fired." Madison turned back to the stove as her employees laughed even harder.

"You should take Sophie up on those shimmy lessons," Miles told her. "Put on some sexy holiday music and give this Chase a private dance. He's on crutches, so he can't escape."

"There's no such thing as sexy holiday music," Madison said but didn't turn around. She could feel the heat that bloomed in her cheeks and didn't want to reveal too much to her annoyingly perceptive employees.

She didn't need any help loosening up. A kiss from Chase had done the job with no problem. If she were any looser, she'd be a boneless heap on the kitchen floor.

The question remained—what was she supposed to do about it? Her choice last night to command him back to his bedroom probably hadn't been advisable.

What if Chase came to his senses and decided that kissing her had been a mistake? Of course, it had been a mistake. But while they were making it, she should have taken more advantage. She should have led him back to her bedroom to scratch the itch that skittered along her spine every time she was close to him. She wanted to chalk up the desire to the long self-imposed drought in the intimacy department she'd been operating under for the past several years.

She knew it was more than that. It was Chase. After all, she worked in the most popular bar and restaurant in Starlight. This was the land of rugged mountain men and sophisticated weekenders who traveled from the city to enjoy the variety of outdoorsy pursuits available in the area.

Plenty of handsome men had darkened Trophy Room's doors in the past. More than a few of them had tried to flirt with her, but she'd either shut them down without a second thought or retreated to the safety of her kitchen.

She wasn't interested in entanglements—romantic or sexual or anywhere in between. So why did her body and heart choose Chase Kent to inspire a reawakening?

No, she reminded herself. Not her heart. The physical attraction she could manage one way or the other. There could be nothing more. She refused to consider anything more, especially with Chase. Was it because he'd admitted to being a bad boy?

She'd always had a weakness for rebels but didn't

believe it about him. He cared about Stella even if, as he said, he didn't want to.

The girl would want to stay with him, flawed and unequipped as he was to raise a teenager. They were family. It wouldn't matter if the cousin in Portland was the perfect mom.

Stella belonged with Chase. Madison had always wanted to have someone to belong to, no matter what. She'd told Chase a bit about her life after her mom died.

She'd failed to mention that she'd made herself scarce so her sister would have a chance at a better life. Jenna was seven years younger than Madison, and they were only half sisters. It would have been too much to expect their mother to stick with the same deadbeat dad.

Madison had been an ill-tempered, angry teenager, but Jenna had been like Stella—a parched desert flower waiting for someone to give her water in the form of love and affection.

When the first social worker who took their case suggested that the girls separate because she had a highly sought-after placement for Jenna, Madison's little sister had grown uncharacteristically stubborn.

She'd refused to go without her older sister. So Madison took off because it was the only way she knew to give Jenna another chance. She understood what Chase wanted to do. But she also understood that Stella needed him.

And Madison needed to focus on keeping herself out of the mix in order to help them stay together.

"There's nothing between Chase and me," she repeated to Sophie and Miles, hoping she'd start to believe it if she said it enough times.

Chapter Eight

An hour later, Madison opened the door to the building that served as Starlight's community center, which hosted art, dance and crafting classes, plus town meetings. The sound of youthful voices joined in the chorus of "Santa Claus Is Coming to Town." She smiled to herself as she thought about how Chase would be handling his role as codirector of the holiday show that she'd volun-told him for.

The man might make her knees go weak, but she still liked the idea of pushing him beyond his comfort level. She knew what it was like to get stuck in old patterns that no longer served. She might not be ready to chair the Starlight Welcome Wagon committee, but she'd come a long way since moving here.

Chase didn't have the time it had taken her to realize he wasn't only an island of a man. She wasn't sure that throwing him into something like a Christmas pageant would turn out to be her best idea, but…

She paused as the music changed, and a deep baritone rose above the other voices.

The song was "White Christmas," and the richness of the soloist's tone made the little hairs on the back of her neck stand on end.

There had to be another man present. She pulled her coat more tightly around herself, despite the sudden heat coursing through her, and moved toward the main room of the center, where the stage had been erected on one side.

To her utter astonishment, Chase stood toward the back of the group of children, taking part in the practice. He'd positioned himself next to Stella, and as she entered, his gaze crashed into hers as he sang the final lines.

"May your days be merry and bright. And may all your Christmases be white."

The heat between them reverberated through her. There was a round of applause from Tessa and the older woman, whom Madison didn't recognize, accompanying the group on the piano.

Tessa announced the end of practice and invited everyone to return to the community center the following afternoon to work on set design. "We're lucky to have Stella's brother, Chase, who not only filled in for Brody on the solo without missing a beat but also happens to be a talented artist."

She pointed at Chase and gave him a wide guileless grin. "I hope that translates into drawing snowflakes and nutcrackers," she told him.

Madison choked back a laugh at his pained expression.

She approached Tessa as the kids dispersed. "You owe me. I got you a volunteer who can sing and draw. You owe me big-time, Tessa."

"Would you say that I owe you or Chase?"

"Madison is the one who owes me," the man in question said as he joined them.

"You sing Christmas songs," she announced with glee.

"You owe me *big-time*."

She gave him a long look, amusement making the corners of her mouth twitch. "I let you move into my home while you recover from a life-threatening accident."

"Then we're even."

"Because you're helping with a local Christmas pageant?"

Before he could answer, a little boy ran up and tugged on his sleeve. "Mr. Chase, you said I couldn't blow my nose in the middle of the song, so I sniffed big and swallowed my boogers. Now they're stuck in my throat. Want to see?"

The kid opened his mouth wide.

"Wow," Chase murmured. "That's incredible."

Tessa grabbed hold of Madison's hand and squeezed. "You can't laugh."

The boy ran off to join his friends.

"Neither of you can laugh at me," Chase warned, shaking his head. "Do you believe we're even now?"

"I haven't shown you my boogers," Madison said solemnly.

Tessa was called over to a group of mothers who'd entered the room.

"You said you're not good with kids." Madison gave Chase a little nudge. She glanced over to the moms who'd gathered nearby. Ella called them the mom posse, and she noticed several of them blatantly staring at Chase.

She didn't know how to describe the feeling that rose inside her other than to call it jealousy, which would be stupid and irresponsible.

One of the mothers, a striking brunette wearing a fitted navy sweaterdress and cute ankle boots, caught her eye. Ignoring Madison's glare, the woman came forward with a wave. "You're the cook from Trophy Room."

"Chef," Madison corrected.

"Sure, sure. I wanted to thank you. We had my brother's engagement party there a few weeks ago. You did an excellent job with the food. I wouldn't normally consider potato skins and hot wings the purview of a chef, but they were that good."

The woman turned toward Chase. "You must be the glass artist? I heard you were in town. I'm Sara Roberts." She held out her hand, which Chase folded into his larger one. Madison suppressed a growl. "It's so scary to think about your accident the way it was described."

"Yeah, it wasn't my finest moment."

"And after you took in your poor orphaned sister."

Madison couldn't help the snort that escaped her mouth. "I thought this was a Santa's toy shop–themed holiday show. Are we going for a Dickens vibe now?"

"I didn't imply that," the woman snapped.

"Right."

"I appreciate your concern," Chase said. "Stella's been through a lot. I want her to be happy."

He gave Madison a pointed look, and she resisted the urge to roll her eyes.

"If there's anything you need while you're in town, we're here for you." Sara took a wallet out of her purse. "I teach a yoga class here at the community center on Saturday mornings. It might be helpful in your recovery. I'm really good with muscles." She handed Chase a business card. "My website and cell number are on there. I have a few free videos you could try at home to get started."

A boy called to her from across the room.

"Coming, Luka, my love." She squeezed Chase's arm and then turned to Madison again. "Great potato skins," she said and sashayed across the room. That woman definitely didn't need shimmy lessons.

"I wonder if she had any particular muscles in mind," Madison muttered.

"A terrifying thought." Chase shoved the card into his back pocket. "Can we get out of here?"

"Wait. You're not interested in her?"

"Are you joking?"

"I just thought…she was so blatant. So obvious."

"Do I seem like a man who would be attracted to blatant and obvious?" He inclined his head. "Because just so we're clear, I'm more into churlish and combative. I'm a masochist that way."

"You also like looking at throat boogers, so I'm not sure about your overall judgment."

"Good point," he conceded with a wry grin. "Thank you, Madison."

The change in his tone made her stomach flutter. "We're even, Chase."

"I don't think so. Stella was nice to me this afternoon."

"Like you said, she's a girl with a good heart."

"I can't figure out teenagers. I guess it's points in my favor that I can carry a tune."

"You're involved in her life right now. That's a win."

His smile faded. "A temporary one."

She didn't want to argue and ruin the moment. It was too precious.

"Well, Mr. Frank Sinatra Pipes, I know what we're not doing tonight."

He gave her a look that did more funny things to her insides. "What's that?"

"Watching yoga videos online."

He threw back his head and laughed, and suddenly Madison couldn't remember why she was so determined to be unaffected by this man.

"I'm not sure this is a great idea," Chase told Tessa and Carson as they drove into town the following night.

"Sure it is," Tessa promised. "Madison will be thrilled to see you."

Carson chuckled and met Chase's gaze in the rearview mirror. "*Thrilled* isn't a word we typically associate with Madison, so that's saying something."

"I highly doubt she'd use that word in association with me," Chase admitted. "More like *irritated* and *impatient*."

Carson laughed at the obvious joke, but Tessa shook her head. "She wouldn't be helping you the way she is if she didn't like you."

"She likes my sister."

Chase wasn't sure why he felt the need to remind them that Madison's help was more about Stella than him. Ever since their kiss, the lines of their arrangement had blurred.

He could think of very little else but pulling Madison into his arms when she was near him, and the proximity they shared in the same house was almost too much to bear.

At the same time, he knew getting involved would be a mistake. She wanted things from him that he couldn't give, and he refused to consider changing his mind. Not about Stella's future or his own.

Watching what he assumed was Stella's usual personality emerge in Starlight was a revelation. Instead of the sulky, disagreeable teen he'd become accustomed to in Seattle, this Starlight version of Stella was sweet and naturally helpful.

It was still hard to believe that Madison, who continued to be gruff and snarky most of the time, had understood that kinder, gentler side of his stepsister was just waiting to be uncovered under the layers of grief and anger she'd draped over herself like armor.

What an embarrassment that Chase had missed it so completely.

He couldn't remember a time when he thought about anything besides himself and his work, to the detriment of everything and everyone else in his life.

He barely had acquaintances, let alone real friendships or relationships. Sure, some people tolerated him—his agent, the gallery owners when he showed his work. But that was because he made them money.

Not one person had called to check on him since his accident.

If Chase couldn't produce, he was useless.

Things were different in Starlight, and not just for Stella.

The people in this town didn't seem to care about his past or his fame or attitude. They accepted the man he was now, mostly broken and unsure how to fix himself.

It couldn't last, of course. His studio was gone, and with it, his purpose in life. He would need to rebuild.

His leg continued to get stronger, and the doctor was happy with how his eye had healed. The scrapes and burns that covered a good portion of his body were lessening, so he needed to overcome the residual trauma of the accident to focus on the future.

Before he could consider what he wanted from it, he had to take care of Stella.

"Do you miss the pace of big-city life?" Carson asked. "Life in a small town can be an adjustment, especially when it's only temporary."

Temporary. That was the reminder Chase needed.

"Even before Stella came to live with me, my life didn't resemble anything typical of a big-city pace. I mostly worked in my studio, unless I was traveling for an installation or opening. I'm solitary by nature."

"Madison said you live outside of Seattle on a few acres," Tessa commented.

The thought that Madison had mentioned him to her friends shouldn't have given him such pleasure. They were probably confirming the veritable stranger staying with her wasn't some kind of creeper. It was apparent the group cared about each other. He couldn't help his jealousy. After all, no one cared for him in that way.

"Yes. It's easier to set up a hot shop in an unincorporated area because of how much natural gas is used."

"What do you like about glass blowing?" Tessa asked like she was truly curious.

"I like the lack of control I have over the glass. I have to find a way to honor it, both when shaping the pieces and adding color. It's a challenge to discover what glass in motion is willing to do."

"I take it safety is also a challenge when working with fire?" Carson raised a brow in the rearview mirror.

Chase's fists clenched, and he forced himself not to overreact to the question. "I can only speak for myself, but I took every safety precaution possible. I still don't understand what caused the explosion. In fact, I need to go into the city in the next couple of days to meet with the fire marshal and insurance adjuster. I want answers."

"Will Madison drive you?" Tessa asked. "Stella is welcome to hang out with us for the day."

"No. Madison has done enough." Chase shook his head. "I'll hire a car."

Carson pulled to a stop a few buildings down from Trophy Room's entrance. Even though it was dark and most of the stores along Starlight's main drag appeared closed for the evening, there were still Christmas lights glowing in almost every window. Strands of lights were also intertwined with greenery draped between lampposts along the sidewalk.

The town looked like a Norman Rockwell–style painting, so Chase was surprised at the inspiration the scene gave him. His creativity had revved up even more since arriving in the small town, which was almost as distracting as the attraction he felt toward Madison.

He'd never taken a break from work, and his muse did not like being ignored.

"I could fly you in," Carson offered as they got out of the truck. "I go to Seattle a few times a week for deliveries and to pick up several local merchants' shipments. Madison is one of them. She has a thing about fresh ingredients."

"I don't want to trouble you," Chase answered automatically.

"It's no trouble. I keep an old truck at one of the regional airfields south of town. I like the freedom when I'm there, so I can drop you at your house before I make my rounds. Look at the timing and let me know what works."

"I will. Thank you." Chase was smart enough not to look a gift horse in the mouth. Part of him had liked the excuse of being stranded in Starlight. The idea of seeing the wreckage of his beloved studio now that he was past the initial shock made his gut twist, but he couldn't avoid it much longer. He followed Tessa and Carson toward the bar. He'd gotten adept enough at walking on crutches to just about keep up. Corners were still tricky, and he'd be grateful when he was cleared to use a cane instead.

They entered the establishment, and he was immediately captivated by the festive atmosphere and updated decor. From the outside, Trophy Room looked like any other small-town dive bar. Inside, it was warm and welcoming, with rustic furniture and vintage posters and photographs of the area hanging on the wood-paneled walls.

There was one display case positioned on a far wall that held a variety of statues, which he assumed were a nod to the bar's name and probably its history within the town.

Chase didn't frequent bars in Seattle, especially since Stella had come to live with him. Before that, he'd only ventured out when his agent or a gallery owner forced him to. Those ventures were to sleek hotel bars or trendy spots where the clientele was painfully self-aware of their status.

This felt more like a family reunion, with several hands going up to greet Tessa and Carson. A tall, burly man Chase assumed was the bar's owner, Jordan Schaeffer, was behind the bar serving patrons.

Another nearly middle-aged blonde, who looked like she'd seen her share of fun, waited on customers at the other end of the bar. It smelled like garlic and tomato sauce and something roasting. Almost every table included not only drinks but food items as well.

Madison had made her mark, although he still wondered about the specifics that had brought her to Starlight. He wanted to hear what had led her to this place in her own words.

Somehow he knew she didn't share the details of her past with many people, so it would mean something if she told him.

"You must be Chase," the bar owner said as Chase approached the long counter.

Tessa and Carson were immediately drawn into a conversation, and Chase didn't relish hovering at the edges like the outsider he was.

"Madison is quite taken with your sister," Jordan said.

Chase ignored the pang of disappointment that stamped at his heart. He wanted her to be taken with him, which was silly.

"She's helped us a lot."

The former football star nodded. "She doesn't like people to know she has a heart, but it's there."

"You've got quite a crowd here tonight. It isn't what I expected."

Jordan flashed a self-satisfied smile. "Trivia night is a weekly tradition. Holiday trivia night draws an even bigger crowd. There are some great prizes up for grabs. My lovely wife outdid herself, soliciting donations from businesses. Each team's entry fee is donated to the community center, so you're still contributing to a good cause if you don't win."

Chase held up a hand. "I'm not playing. Stella is babysitting for Carson and Tessa, and they were nice enough to insist I come with them. I'm another few weeks from being released to drive."

Jordan grabbed a piece of paper tacked to a bulletin board behind the bar. "It says right here you're on team Naughty Elves. That's our in-house team, comprised of Madison and her kitchen staff. They lost to the hospital group last year by only three points. My chef is a sore loser. I hope you know your holiday trivia, because she has high expectations."

"I hardly bother to celebrate Christmas," Chase admitted.

Jordan made a face. "This should be fun."

"I thought Madison was working tonight." Chase glanced around but had a feeling she wasn't among the crowd. His body wasn't going haywire like it normally did when she was close.

"We shut down the kitchen extra early on trivia night," Jordan told him. "You'll do fine as long as Madison wins."

At that moment, a swinging door he assumed led to the kitchen opened, and two people in costumes filed out. The crowd cheered. Then the excitement grew more palpable as a third person appeared in the doorway.

Chase felt a grin split his face at the sight of Madison in a green-and-red-striped elf costume that matched her staff's, along with a pointed hat. Twin spots of pink colored her cheeks, and she looked like she wanted to murder every person staring at her.

Then her gaze met his.

Chapter Nine

Madison walked toward Chase, the noise of the crowded bar dissolving into the background as his enigmatic gaze held hers.

"Nice hat," he said, reaching up to flick the silver bell fastened to the tip. "I'm getting real North Pole vibes from you." His mouth curved up at the edges. "Other than your facial expression, which gives the impression that you stepped in a pile of dog poo on the way over here."

"I'm glad you like that hat so much." She gave him a smug smile and then thrust the elf hat Sophie had handed her into his lap. "Put this on."

"No, thank you."

"You have to wear it," Miles said as he came to

stand on Chase's other side. "You're a Naughty Elf now."

"An aspiration I didn't even realize I had." Chase turned toward Miles. "Chase Kent."

"I know," Madison's employee said with a smirk. "I've heard all about you."

"That's an exaggeration," she felt compelled to point out.

Miles introduced himself, and the two men shook hands. Chase seemed calmer than she would have expected in this situation and responded with aplomb to a few more of Miles's teasing jabs.

He donned the elf hat, which should have looked ridiculous. She knew it did on her. But the green and red felt with the bell dangling from the tip did nothing to diminish Chase's masculine appeal.

She had a feeling he'd look hot in a full-on Santa suit.

"How are you at trivia?" Miles asked.

Chase grimaced. "Pathetic."

"Deadweight," Madison muttered. "Perfect."

Chase smiled like she'd made some hilarious joke. She was using snark to put emotional distance between them, and the fact that he wasn't rising to her bait didn't comfort her. She felt even more off balance than when her friends surrounded her, but Chase's presence gave her the sensation of finally belonging.

"That's okay." Miles patted Chase's shoulder. "The

Tool Cool for Yule team from the hospital won last year. They're our biggest threat, and a couple of the nurses keep glancing over at you like they're staring at the dessert buffet. Your job is going to be to distract them when the questions start. Smile, wink, take off your shirt if you're so inclined…"

"I'm not," Chase said.

"Pity," Miles answered with a pout. "We're going to have to rely on your bedroom eyes." He waved when someone called his name from the back of the bar. "We've got twenty minutes until the first round. Madi, loosen up but not too much. We need you in top form tonight. One of the prizes is a night at a four-star hotel in Seattle, and I promised my boyfriend I'd take him into the city for our anniversary."

Chase stared as Miles walked away and then turned to Madison. "He wasn't serious about the shirt, right?"

Her mouth spread into a genuine smile. "Probably, although I don't think he'd be offended if you changed your mind." She glanced over her shoulder to confirm that the women from the hospital were indeed keeping their gazes trained on Chase. "First, the yoga instructor. Now the nurses. You don't get out much in Starlight, but you sure make it count when you do."

"I'm not making anything count."

She tapped a finger on her chin, entertained by his agitation. "Is it the brooding artist energy or the thought of helping a wounded man recover that appeals to them? I wonder." Her finger reached out to touch his cheek as if by its own accord. "Maybe it's the dimple."

"I haven't smiled at either of those women. They don't know about the dimple." He grabbed her hand when she started to lower it. "I'm saving my smiles for you."

Prickly heat raced through her, but she didn't let it show on her face. "I'm honored."

"I want to kiss you again."

She looked around to make sure no one had heard his words. "You can't say that. We agreed it's a bad idea."

"I didn't agree to anything," he told her.

"But you know it's true."

"Maybe we could both use trouble in the form of a release."

She knew he was talking about physically. In some ways, that appealed to her more than she cared to admit. Her life mainly had changed for the better, but there were moments she missed the adrenaline rush that her previous bad habits had given her.

She had no desire or intention to revisit her former vices, but Chase was more dangerous and thrilling than any buzz a substance could give her. She liked him, not just because he was physically perfect, although that was very much the case.

She liked his imperfections and how he wore them like a badge of honor. He didn't try to be someone he wasn't. Still, there was more to him than he gave himself credit for.

"It's a bad idea," she repeated.

That dimple flashed. "You like bad ideas. Being bad makes you feel good. I can make you feel very good, Madison."

The promise in his words made her stomach swoop like a red-tailed hawk circling the quiet valley. She'd done an excellent job of ignoring her baser urges and natural propensity for trouble since coming to Starlight. She hid behind the mask of bristly sarcasm because pretending was easier than allowing emotion in that she might not be able to control.

Perhaps being bad with Chase was a good idea after all. A test of sorts. She knew he was leaving along with Stella. Even if she let herself fall for him— and she wasn't sure she could resist— there was no way it would or could last.

The end might wreck her, but she'd allow herself the time to lick her wounds and move on. It would be a way to prove to herself that she could also handle more than she gave herself credit for.

"We need to win trivia night first." She brushed his knee with hers, and the heat between them felt like it had the potential to flare out of control like a forest fire.

Madison ignored the warning bells in her brain. She might have turned over several new leaves since coming to Starlight, but she still gravitated toward self-destructive behavior. "It's important to Miles and Sophie."

"But not you?"

She let her knee press harder against his. "I like to come out on top."

His nostrils flared, and those thundercloud eyes went even darker. Madison enjoyed teasing him with the innuendo and his reaction to the underlying meaning of her words.

"Then be prepared to see my dimple do its thing," he said, his voice pitched low like he was sharing a secret.

She nodded. "I can hardly wait."

"I can't believe they gave me fifty dollars," Stella said later that night from the back seat of Madison's SUV.

"They were grateful to have you stay with Lauren," Madison told the girl. "She likes you a lot."

"I would have done it for a lot less. She's sweet and so easy. We did spa things, and then she read to me. I guess Tessa told her that she has to read *Little Women* before they watch the movie. It sounds like something my mom would have made me do. She used to say that books are better and didn't want the movie version to ruin it for me."

Madison sucked in a breath as the girl's voice turned wistful. "Dad used to read to me every night. He did the best voices."

Madison tried not to outwardly react to Stella's words for fear she would stop sharing. She hadn't heard the teen talk in any detail about her parents before this. Glancing out of the corner of her eye, she noted Chase's shocked expression.

It appeared this was also new territory for him.

"Did Dad read to you when you were little?" Stella asked her brother.

A muscle ticked in Chase's jaw, but his tone was gentle when he answered, "Not that I remember."

"He did great voices," the girl repeated.

Madison filled the silence that ensued by telling Stella how Chase had come up with the final answer that helped their team clinch the holiday trivia competition.

"How did you know that roast duck is the most popular menu item at Christmas in Germany?"

One big shoulder lifted, then lowered. "I had a German apprentice a few years ago. She talked way too much about holiday traditions."

"I'm gathering you didn't have much to add to that conversation," Madison suggested.

"Nada," he said with a dry chuckle. "I tried not to retain any of the drivel she shared. I guess a few random facts wormed their way into my memory."

"A boon for Team Naughty Elves."

"Plus, you got this awesome prize basket," Stella added.

"She gave away the good stuff to her staff," Chase told his sister.

"But kept the cookies and hot cocoa bombs," Stella countered. "Works for me."

Chase grumbled, but Madison knew he supported her decision to share the best parts of the prize with Sophie and Miles.

He'd been a surprisingly good sport and a fierce competitor during the rounds of trivia. Both Sophie and Miles had been giddy over Chase's blatant flirting with women from the other teams, giving them a clear advantage.

They returned to the house, and Stella headed to her room. Madison wasn't sure what happened next. She wanted the good time that Chase had promised. She wanted more, if she were being totally honest.

But Stella wasn't necessarily asleep, though she'd gone to her bedroom. Besides, Madison and Chase weren't a real couple. She had no idea how to handle being alone with him, given her feelings and desire.

"Your mind is working overtime," he told her as he rested his crutches against the island and took his usual seat.

"Would you like a glass of water?"

"Sure." He smiled like he knew exactly why she was making the offer—distraction. "Is it hard to work in a bar and be around the alcohol?"

She stilled. She'd heard the question before and knew the easy answer. It surprised her that he'd asked it, especially at this moment, since talking about her struggles with alcohol wouldn't be considered fore-play for either of them.

"I thought I'd struggle with it. In fact, I took the position because I wanted to challenge myself. I wanted to punish myself." She filled two tumblers with water and placed one on the counter in front of Chase. "I was angry and filled with regret for what happened when I hit rock bottom."

He raised a brow.

"Oh, so you want the gory details?"

"Not if you don't want to share," he told her.

She found she didn't mind the thought of him knowing. "I was good at hiding my drinking and managed to be a high-functioning drunk, as much as there can be such a thing. A few years ago, my younger sister reached out to me. Jenna and I lost touch for a while because she was taken in by one of our relatives after Mom died."

"You weren't?"

She shook her head. "No, which was part of why I disappeared from her life, but she never gave up on me. I love her. I wanted to see her. I needed to have that connection and know that somebody gave a fig about me, even though I couldn't care less about my-self. We'd made plans to be together for Christmas, but she came to the restaurant and told me that her foster mom had been diagnosed with cancer. The family planned a last-minute trip for the holidays because they didn't know how long she had. I understood, but..."

"You still felt betrayed."

"I felt like she was choosing them over me. Like her big talk about us reconnecting was just talk. She wanted me in her life when it was convenient for her. Family isn't convenient. I was mad and stormed out of the kitchen to my car. Normally, I was smart enough to walk or take a taxi home when I'd overserved myself during a shift. At that moment, I just wanted to get away. She hopped in the car with me. I told her not to. I screamed and said horrible things, but she said we would work through it. She wasn't giving up on me. If Christmas meant that much, she would find a way to make it work. Then I took the exit ramp off the highway too fast and hit the curb. The car flipped."

Madison drew in a shaky breath. "And flipped again. I walked away, and she didn't. She had a broken pelvis and internal injuries, mostly to her reproductive organs. The doctors said we were lucky she didn't bleed out right there on the side of the highway with a drunk sister puking her guts out a few feet away. I could barely hold her hand while we waited for an ambulance because I was drunk and I was sick and..." She shook her head. "I don't deserve her love."

"I've met your sister," Chase said. "When Stella got in trouble and was ordered mandatory community service, I talked to several nonprofits to decide which would be the best fit. Jenna impressed me with her dedication and her vision for helping teenagers."

"Jenna is amazing," Madison agreed. "I don't know how she turned out so well after being let down by almost everyone in her life."

"You got sober after the accident?" he asked.

"Yes." She took a long drink of water to soothe her suddenly dry throat. "Immediately. It's also when I left Seattle. I'm not sure if I was trying to reinvent myself as much as running away from who I'd been. Either way, I saw an ad to run the kitchen at Trophy Room and ended up in Starlight."

"So something good came from the accident in the end?"

"When you hit literal rock bottom, there's no place to go but up." She laughed softly. "This isn't exactly sexy-times talk. If you were smart, my sad story would send you running in the opposite direction."

He crooked a finger. "Come over here, Madison."

"I don't like being told what to do."

"Take pity on the man with the injured leg."

She moved around the island. He reached out and tugged her to him when she was close enough. "Being smart is different than being bad." He nuzzled the crook of her neck. "Just to be clear, I know the difference. They aren't mutually exclusive."

"I hope you're right," she said, then moaned as he nibbled on a particularly sensitive spot near her earlobe.

He threaded his strong hands through her hair and kissed her. They stayed like that for several moments, savoring each other. Chase's hands moved over her body like he wanted to learn every inch of her.

Madison quickly broke away at the sound of a toilet flushing from upstairs in the house.

"She's not going to come down." Chase's voice was scratchy, and his chest rose and fell like he was having trouble drawing in a full breath. It was gratifying to know that he was as affected by their kisses as she felt.

Still, she took another step away. "We can't risk it. Stella is the priority for both of us."

"She likes you."

That made Madison's heart tug. "I'm going to bed alone," she said.

He let out one of those growls she was coming to love.

Her mouth turned up at one corner. "Don't be surprised if I accidentally sleepwalk my way into your room tonight."

He flashed a grin, then shook his head. "No accident, Madison. When you come to me, I want you to do it on purpose. I want you to choose."

She nodded and bit down on her lower lip. "I'll choose you, Chase," she said, then headed for her room.

Chapter Ten

Chase couldn't believe he'd drifted off to sleep with the promise of Madison paying him a late-night visit. The day must have made him more exhausted than he cared to admit, because he blinked awake with a start in his darkened room at the feel of her long fingers moving across his bare chest.

"I hope I'm not interrupting a good dream," she said against his ear.

Desire spiraled through him as her breath tickled his skin. "You're better than any dream."

He felt her go still. "I'm no one's better, Chase."

"Madison." He reached out an arm and wrapped it around her, lifting her until she was straddling him. "Are you wearing one of my T-shirts?" he asked, momentarily confused by the fact that she'd climbed into his bed with most of her body covered.

She huffed out a laugh. "I left my robe on the floor by the door, but then I felt weird about being in just my underpants. It's been a while since... I used to be braver with liquid courage running through my veins."

"You don't need that," he said, then tugged on the hem of the shirt. "Or this. For the record..." He lifted the soft fabric up and over her head, then lost his entire train of thought—along with most of his brain cells—at the sight of her pale skin in the dim glow from the streetlight coming through the slats of the blinds.

Her breasts were perfect, the right size to fit in his hands, with rosy tips. As he watched her, they puckered, and he felt himself grow inexorably harder in response.

"For the record?" she repeated on a husky breath as he skimmed his thumbs over her breasts.

He forced his fuzzy mind to focus. "You don't have to be better than anything or anyone with me. I happen to like you just the way you are."

"That's the nicest thing I've heard in a long time." Her breath hitched as he lifted his head far enough to lick one perfect tip. "Does that say more about me or you?"

"You know what makes my glass sculptures so popular?"

"Mmm..."

"The details in them." He swirled his tongue over her smooth skin. She tasted like apples and sunshine. How was that possible? "I use what some people consider imperfections to make my pieces unique. It's all perspective."

She placed her hands on either side of his face and lifted it to kiss him, tracing her tongue across the seam of his lips. He circled her waist with his hands, loving how she fit in his grasp.

"My perspective," she said as she cupped his jaw, "is that you're talking too much."

"I respect that," he said, then tried to hide his wince as he moved too sharply, pain firing through his leg.

Madison immediately went still. "Is this too much? We can—"

"It's fine," he said on a slow sigh. "I'm going to need to rely on you to take the lead here." He made a show of flopping his arms wide. "Have your merry way with me, so to speak."

"Less speaking," she reminded him. "More merry."

That was exactly what happened next as Madison drove him to the edge of desire with her clever hands and her wicked mouth.

Chase wasn't used to giving up control in any area of his life, and certainly not the bedroom. But he found he liked relinquishing power to her. He liked her confidence in exploring his body and the way she gave soft commands about how she wanted to be touched in return.

By the time she'd stripped them both naked, his body was practically pulsing with need. Well, certain parts were already pulsing.

So when she rolled a condom over his length and then lowered herself onto him, it felt like every single dream he'd had in his life coming true. It felt like coming home, which was ridiculous.

He knew great sex didn't symbolize more than a physical release.

But his heart lurched as Madison moved on top of him, looking every inch of the goddess he knew her to be. He wrapped his arms tightly around her and their mouths melded, tongues mimicking their body movements.

It was a heady sensation—made even more potent because his heart seemed as engaged as his body. When they found their releases, her first with him quickly following, it was like a million stars exploding behind his eyes and in his heart.

As much as Chase would have liked to deny it, he knew this woman was changing everything for him.

Chase stood in the burned-out remains of his studio two days later, his stomach tied in knots as he surveyed the destruction. At the same time, he realized how much worse it could have been.

He'd been knocked backward by the initial explosion and had lost consciousness for what he assumed was close to a full minute. If Stella hadn't been home and come running to find him, practically dragging him from the burning building, who knew what would have happened?

He wanted to believe he would have gotten out on his own, but now he understood how bad the damage was and questioned his ability to survive the blast and fire.

Viewing the scene without a concussion and the numbing benefit of the heavy-duty pain meds the docs had prescribed him gave a new perspective on how a different outcome might have impacted his stepsister.

She'd lost both of her parents in a fiery car accident. While she didn't openly talk about the similarities between the two events, he couldn't help but think it weighed on her.

He would have to call the therapist who had been recommended when she first came to live with him and thought it a miracle she hadn't acted out more since his accident. Instead, she seemed to be in the best mood since their time together.

That could be attributed to Starlight, and more specifically to Madison, who could also take credit for giving Chase the unfamiliar feeling of contentment he now had. This trip into the city was a harsh reminder that it couldn't last. He had to rebuild. There were commissions and obligations and life in Seattle. Nothing about his previous life seemed appealing at the moment.

"What caused the initial explosion?"

Chase turned to face Carson Campbell as the pilot entered the studio. After landing at the airstrip outside town, he'd driven Chase to his house. Chase had spent a couple of hours on his own before the insurance adjuster arrived.

"We believe it was debris stuck in one of the blowpipes," the thin, gray-haired man told Carson now.

"That's impossible," Chase said, not sure if he was trying to convince the other men or himself. "I keep my bench in perfect condition. One of the first lessons in glass blowing is how to take care of the equipment, so an accident doesn't happen." He shook his head. "I take every precaution, so it still doesn't make any sense."

The initial explosion lit a stack of newspapers on fire, and the flames spread too fast.

Carson moved farther into the studio. Between the devastation from the explosion, the fire and the water damage, the place was a mess. It would have to be razed entirely and rebuilt.

"If Chase says he took safety precautions," Carson said with a nod, "there must be another explanation."

It was interesting to have a man who didn't know him well stick up for him.

"Sometimes people get careless." The fire chief placed a hand on the charred annealer, the final furnace used to cool the glass. Chase had owned his current model since the start of his career, and it pained him to think of starting over.

"I don't get careless," Chase answered.

"You have apprentices who work with you. Maybe one of them?" The insurance adjuster continued to make notes on the tablet he held. Chase had the urge to smash the thing over the man's head.

"No one else was here the day of the accident. We've been over this."

The fire chief raised a bushy eyebrow. "Who else had access to the space?"

"No one."

"We're not ruling out arson," the burly man said slowly, and Chase felt his whole body tense. "You take care of your stepsister. She got in trouble with the high school for starting a fire."

"That was accidental," Chase snapped. "A firework that went awry. Are you implying that my sister tried to burn me to a crisp but thought better of it and came out to rescue me?"

"I'm just looking for answers," the fire chief told him.

"Nobody wants answers more than me. You're asking the wrong questions about the wrong people and wasting my time. I can't work without a studio, so I need the insurance money."

"You'll get it," the adjuster said, "once our investigation is complete."

Chase started to growl, and his mind immediately

strayed to how much Madison liked to comment on his guttural sounds. He didn't want to think about her in this moment of rage he had no place to stow away.

The studio contained a decade's worth of items, and while he wasn't a sentimental man, the loss overwhelmed him. There was no way Stella could be involved.

He forced himself to draw in a slow breath. "I need a minute," he said through gritted teeth to no one in particular. "I'll be back."

Without waiting for an answer, he limped out. Entering the house from the open garage, he moved into the kitchen and gripped the counter's edge until the feeling of panic subsided. He lifted his head to glance around his open-concept first floor, seeing the space as Stella might view it.

A black leather couch and matching chairs were arranged in the family room with a copper coffee table and a flat-screen television hanging on the wall. His kitchen was sleek and industrial in appliances and cabinetry with stark white stone countertops. The home was sparse compared to either Madison's eclectic decor or the cozy rancher where Stella had lived with her parents. Regret tumbled through him like a rock slide hammering down a cliff. He should have done better by his sister. She'd taken only her possessions from her family home, and Chase had paid to have the rest boxed up and put into storage.

He'd packed away her previous life and expected

her to fit into his. No wonder she didn't feel comfortable inviting friends, a teenage girl forced to live in a bachelor's cheerless and uninviting home.

For years, Chase had only given his emotions to his work, never considering the idea that the life he lived outside of the studio was just as much a measure of his worth as the sculptures he created.

Could he even figure out a way to find a better balance? If he stopped dedicating everything to his art, would his creativity suffer? An age-old dilemma he didn't know how to answer.

"How are you doing?"

Chase turned as Carson walked through the door from the garage.

He thought about lashing out. Obviously, he wasn't doing okay, but he was sick of pretending to be. Tired of being alone with no support system in his life other than the people he paid.

"I keep thinking about what could have happened if I hadn't made it out. I'm responsible for Stella. A car accident is tragic, but knowing I've been careless without realizing it is killing me. What if there had been a second explosion when she came to find me? My stepsister walked into a burning building because I was in there. It's equally humbling and terrifying."

"I crashed my plane last year."

Chase blinked, shock reverberating through him.

"Lauren had just come to live with me full-time, and I wasn't handling it well. I made a rash decision to fly in conditions that weren't ideal. I know better. I managed to land the plane in an open meadow. The thought of almost losing both my daughter and Tessa still haunts me."

Carson moved closer, and Chase could feel the tension coming from him. "I made changes after that, and not only doubling down on my safety protocols. I changed how I value people who are important to me. Losing your studio is a blow, but you can recover from it. What comes next now that you've been given another chance?"

Chase smothered a bewildered laugh. "You might be going too deep for a guy like me."

"I am full of wisdom," Carson said with a quick grin. "You could learn a lot from me—just don't tell Tessa I said so."

"I wish I were a better student."

"You've heard the message. It's up to you to decide what to do with it."

Chase's cousin Brandie had responded last night to his email about Stella. She was willing to consider taking in the girl and wanted to talk in more detail. Today was a reminder that he wasn't equipped to give his stepsister what she needed.

Maybe Carson was right, and Chase could learn, grow and make it work. Or perhaps it would be better for all of them if he gave Stella a new start.

"I'm going to head back out to the studio." Chase glanced at his watch. "Can you give me another half hour?"

Carson nodded. "I have some calls to make. We'll head out when you're ready and be home in time for dinner."

Home.

The word had never held much meaning for Chase, but now the thought of returning to Madison and Stella made his heart stutter. It was becoming more challenging to find the energy to fight for his solitary life, and he suddenly wished he could be the type of man worthy of something more.

Chapter Eleven

Madison walked into her house a few minutes after eight o'clock that night and stopped short in the laundry room just off the garage.

She could hear the television from the family room and the scent of the enchiladas she'd left in the refrigerator for Chase to heat.

It was such a change from the silence that typically greeted her since she was often the last one to leave the Trophy Room kitchen. They stopped serving food at 8:00 p.m. on weeknights, but she readily found excuses to stick around and get prep done for the following day. Sometimes she focused on extra cleaning.

She might have the cleanest commercial kitchen in Washington State.

Being busy at the bar was preferable to coming home to her quiet, dark house. Even after installing lights timed to brighten the interior for her arrival, emptiness seemed to permeate every corner.

She liked to pretend she enjoyed being alone—and often she did. But as her friends in town had partnered off with their respective boyfriends and husbands, her solitary existence impacted her in a different way.

Tonight, she'd been distracted to the point that she'd nearly sliced off the tip of her pinkie finger. Madison didn't make those kinds of mistakes.

Miles and Sophie had finally confronted her on her odd behavior. Old Madison had wanted to lash out and tell them to mind their own business.

New Madison, the one she was coming to like more every day, admitted that her thoughts were consumed with Chase and his visit to Seattle. He'd sent a few terse texts throughout the day, letting her know he and Carson had arrived safely and their timing for returning to Starlight.

She imagined it had to be as strange for him to share his schedule as it was for her on the receiving end of the updates.

She liked it.

She liked him more than was healthy for her equilibrium.

After their night together, she wanted to believe he was out of her system, but that was nowhere near the case. She'd purposely stayed away until after midnight the previous evening because she didn't want to come off looking needy if he didn't want a repeat engagement.

To her shock, he'd been waiting for her when she got home smelling like the garlic chicken special at the bar with her feet aching. She'd tried to protest, but he'd led her into the small bathroom connected to the guest bedroom, obviously frustrated that his injury prevented him from joining her in the shower.

Instead, he'd sat on the closed toilet seat and peppered her with questions about her evening like they were a real couple.

It had felt real to her.

Even more so when he wrapped her in a fluffy towel to dry and then rubbed lotion all over her body. By the time they'd made it to the bed, she was equally aroused and relaxed. Their joining had been different from the first time—unhurried in the manner of a couple who knew how to please each other.

The sex was amazing. The connection she felt to him was much more.

She hadn't protested tonight when Miles and Sophie insisted she leave work early to check in with Chase after his trip.

Madison never left work early.

She walked into her kitchen, wondering if Chase or Stella would think it strange that she was there.

"You're home," Stella announced with a smile as she pounded down the steps. "Those enchiladas were so good. Would you teach me how to make the sauce? My mom always said she was going to learn every fall when the roasters sold bags of chilies from their stalls at the farmers' market. She never got around to it."

"Um, sure." Stella's enthusiasm was a different kind of strange. The teen's mood continued to be a mystery to Madison, but she loved how Stella was becoming more comfortable talking about her parents.

She glanced toward the kitchen to see Chase staring at the two of them with a frown. It wasn't easy for him to hear Stella talk about her parents, especially his father, when Chase's relationship with Martin Kent had been so different from his stepsister's.

"I'm glad you liked the enchiladas. The secret to green chili is cooking it low and slow. That's the key to a lot of sauces."

"Low and slow," Stella repeated with a nod. "Can I go to the winter mixer at the high school Saturday night?" The girl addressed the question to Madison, even though Chase was standing right there. "Brody texted and invited me. He wants to introduce me to some of his friends."

Madison felt her mouth drop open, and she quickly shut it and schooled her features. "That's for you and Chase to decide."

"You don't care, right?" Stella's gaze swung to her stepbrother. "It will be great to have me out of your hair for the night. No pretending like you want to hang out with me instead of sulking on the couch, staring at your leg." She crossed her arms over her chest. "Which I know you blame me for."

Madi turned to face Chase, who looked as pole-axed as she felt by the girl's whiplash-fast change of mood and topic. "Low and slow," she whispered.

To her surprise, his expression remained blank, although sparks simmered in his stormy eyes.

"Why would I blame you?" His hands clenched into fists at his sides. He wore cargo pants and an olive-colored Henley, his dark hair rumpled and stubble shadowing his jaw. He looked equal parts tired and exasperated. "You saved my life after the explosion."

"Your life wasn't in danger." Stella's tone had taken on a desperate, reedy thread. "You would have been fine." She glared at his leg like she could will it to heal just by the force of her gaze. "You will be fine. Back to normal."

"Not normal." He rubbed his hand against his thigh. "I'll likely always walk with a limp. It's going to take a long time to rebuild my studio once the in-surance money comes through. I'm not even sure where to start, and today left me with more questions than answers."

"What did the adjuster and the fire chief have to report?" Madison asked before Stella could fire back another aggressive response. It was comical to think of Madison as a mediator, but that was the role she often seemed to take with her two houseguests.

Just when she thought the Kents were making progress and bridging the emotional chasm between them, they'd have a little dustup, as often instigated by Stella as Chase.

"The fire chief mentioned arson," Chase reported like he was discussing the weather.

Madison heard Stella's gasp and felt as shocked as the teen. "Who would do that?"

"Maybe a former apprentice I let go or verbally harangued. It feels unlikely. They're grasping at straws." Chase massaged a hand over his neck like he was trying to work out a knot.

"Is it possible you have legitimate enemies?"

"I didn't think so. My reputation is as a demanding teacher and exacting boss, but I'm not a bad guy. My students and colleagues like me."

"Being demanding is not the worst thing in the world," Madison muttered, thinking how many of her former employees would describe her the same way.

Chase's shoulders lowered slightly as if the fact they had that in common gave him comfort.

"Apparently, someone disagrees. The studio is a wreck, but they found debris shoved in the blowpipe that could have caused an explosion. They wanted to blame me, but my safety precautions are solid." His chest rose and fell in a labored breath. "If they discover this wasn't an accident, I'm going to—"

"It was me," Stella yelled suddenly. She stomped forward and thrust out her hands in front of her. "Call the cops. Have me arrested. It's my fault your studio burned to the ground."

A chill tracked along Madison's spine, and she felt her knees lock at the girl's confession.

Chase stared at his sister, then took a slow hop forward. His face had lost its blank expression, and now he positively glowered as emotion—dark and fiery—radiated from him.

"We should sit down," Madison suggested.

"Explain," Chase commanded Stella.

The word was spoken on such a fierce growl it conjured up images in Madison's mind of a grizzly bear.

"I didn't mean it." Tears ran down Stella's pale cheeks. "The guys wanted to see the equipment."

"You let your friends into my studio? You don't have a key."

"You always leave it in the pocket of the canvas jacket you wear when you're working."

Madison had a vision of the bag of Chase's ruined clothes the hospital had given her when he'd been discharged. She remembered seeing the tan jacket with a leather collar. The scent of acrid smoke had permeated everything, and she'd decided to throw it all away.

"You went through my pockets and broke into the studio?" His face seemed to grow fiercer with every passing second. "You let your delinquent friends touch my stuff? Do you know how expensive some of that equipment is? How delicate?" He rubbed a hand over the top of his thigh. "How dangerous?"

"I'm sorry, okay?" As Chase's voice rose to a thundering pitch, Stella looked like she was shrinking in on herself.

"Who was in my studio?"

"Me, Joey and Hunter." Stella dashed a hand over her cheeks. "I know it was dumb, but it got weird in the house. Hunter wanted to siphon off your liquor, and then Joey tried to kiss me. I didn't know how to handle it. Despite what you think, I'm not having sex with anyone."

"You weren't supposed to have friends at my house when I wasn't home."

"No one wants to come over while you're there when you're always so rude."

"Because your so-called friends are trash," he argued.

"Chase, stop. I know you're mad, but you don't want to do this." Madison felt like she was standing in the bright lights of a runaway train. He hadn't looked like this since they'd arrived in Starlight that first week.

He and Stella could not revert to how bad things had been between them after all their progress. Madison was familiar with the defense mechanism of lashing out when emotions got the best of her. She couldn't imagine how she would feel if she'd lost her kitchen and discovered someone's carelessness had caused the damage.

Chase ignored her warning as he wagged a finger at his stepsister. "I told you before—"

"I know." Stella held up a hand. "If I hang out with trash, pretty soon, I'm going to stink. I'm surprised you haven't been able to smell me before now. Those were my friends in Seattle because everybody else thought I was weird. If they were nice to me, my bad luck would rub off on them and their parents were going to die, too. They didn't know how to deal with me any more than you did. I'm sorry I'm the worst sister in the world. I'm sorry I wasn't the one in that explosion instead of you."

Stella broke off when the sobs racking her body became too much to speak around. Madison waited for Chase to offer some comfort. As angry as he was, she knew he wouldn't have wanted Stella hurt. She hoped, somewhere deep inside, the girl realized that as well.

Now he had to confirm it. Only he didn't. His mouth went even tighter. "You should have told me right away. How am I supposed to trust you after this? What do I tell my insurance about the fire?"

Give the man an award for stupidity in dealing with a devastated teenage girl. Not that his sentiment was wrong, but Stella wasn't a normal teen who'd gotten into trouble.

As happy as she seemed here in Starlight and as

resilient as she wanted people to believe she was, Madison knew the girl was fragile at her core.

She expected Stella to fight back, but she didn't. It broke Madison's stalwart heart.

"I'm sorry," she whispered, then ran back up the stairs to her room.

When Madison heard the door slam above them, she turned to face Chase fully. "You have to make this better."

He gaped at her. "Better how? You heard what she said. I could have been killed. She could have been killed."

"I'm not saying there shouldn't be consequences." She wasn't sure what she was saying. All she knew was that when she'd acted out as a teenager, there had been nobody to tell her she was better than the scum she believed herself to be. She didn't want Stella ever to doubt she was loved.

"She has to know you love her. You can be mad, but it's important that—"

"Don't tell me how I'm allowed to feel or need to act," he snapped, his voice tight.

"I'm trying to help. I know what it's like to be a girl who doesn't feel like she has anyone."

"You and Stella do not have the same situation. She had parents who loved her. She had a father figure who loved her, unlike me…unlike you. You are not her mother, Madison."

Her head snapped back from his words, which felt as sharp as any physical slap.

"I'm not trying to make either of you believe that I am."

"Stella can think about her actions in her room all night if that's what she wants. You want us to have something in common—there you go. We agree that we make each other miserable."

"No." Madison's rational mind understood that he was being cruel because he was hurt, angry and scared. It didn't make her feel better or stop her from questioning whether she'd made a horrible mistake opening herself up to Chase and Stella.

Her life might feel empty on her own, but she knew how to deal with loneliness. It was like an old friend, the most dependable one she had and the only thing she could depend on. Opening her life and heart had proved that it only ended in hurt and heartache.

"Enjoy your anger," she told Chase.

She wished she'd stayed in town until the bar closed and minded her own business. She wished she could pretend like she didn't care. "I hope it keeps you warm tonight."

Chase spent hours trying to fall asleep as Madison's words rang through his head like the most annoying holiday song he'd ever heard.

The image of Stella with tears running down her face caused his stomach to churn with guilt.

His sister had made another mistake, this one nearly catastrophic. He could hold her responsible, but it wasn't fair to blame her for not admitting it to him outright.

Since she'd come to live with him, he'd given her no reason to trust his reaction to anything.

He might not like her friends, but her explanation for why those were the people she chose to hang out with broke his heart. Things had changed for them both since arriving in Starlight.

As angry as he was about what she'd done, he didn't want to lose the gains he'd made in their relationship.

How in the hell was Madison so damn wise when it came to him and Stella?

He'd also been brutish to Madison, and she deserved an apology from him. They both did. At two in the morning, he climbed out of bed, grabbed his crutches after throwing on a sweatshirt and made his way through the quiet house.

Madison had left the Christmas tree on in the front window, the lights giving the darkened space a hopeful glow.

He wanted to believe it was a sign, but by the time he'd made it to the second floor, silently scooting up the steps one at a time so as not to wake his sister, he was achy, sweating and annoyed. His strength was improving, his recovery progressing at the pace the doctor wanted. Still, his physical weakness was another irritation in what felt like an avalanche of frustrations trying to bury him.

He had to try to make it better. Chase might not be perfect, but he had to try.

Of course, he wouldn't have expected Madison to come to him tonight with how they'd left things. But the stubborn, abandoned boy inside of him wanted her to. He wanted her to give him the unconditional support she expected him to offer Stella.

As he limped down the hallway, he tried not to consider what it said about him that he was sneaking up to Madison's bedroom in the wee hours. The sad boy inside him would have to wait his damn turn.

He paused outside the door to the office that served as Stella's bedroom during their stay. When she'd first come to live with him, he looked in on his sister almost every night to watch her sleeping, the way a parent of a small child would.

He'd needed reassurance that she was safe in her bed and had still been somewhat unable to believe he had responsibility for her.

Martin Kent had spent Chase's whole life making him feel not good enough. Why would he have put him in charge of the girl Chase knew Martin considered his precious daughter in every way that counted?

As he peered into the room, it felt like a throwback to those early nights. Except Stella's bed was empty. He paused and listened to see if he could hear her. Maybe she'd come out and fallen asleep on the couch, and he'd missed it. Maybe she was in the bathroom. Maybe…

"Stella?" he called, turning to peer down the hallway as panic gripped his chest. "Stella, where are you? Answer me right now. Stella?"

A moment later, a sleepy Madison appeared in the doorway of the master bedroom at the end of the hall. "What's going on? What time is it?"

"Is Stella in there with you?"

Madison shook her head. "I haven't seen her since she stormed out of the kitchen earlier."

"Stella," he yelled again. There was no answer. "I can't…" He shook his head and turned for the steps. "Do you think she's gone?"

"Gone," Madison repeated like she was trying to make sense of his words. "Where would she have gone?"

"We have to search the house. I need to find her." He started down the hall but realized too late that he'd forgotten to put his weight on the crutches. He lurched forward and caught himself just before he went down.

Madison's arms came around him, offering the support he'd wanted earlier. Not now.

Now he understood he didn't matter. Only Stella. He looked into Madison's blue eyes, searching for the strength he didn't have at the moment. "We have to find her."

"We will." She hurried down the steps, leaving him gasping for breath around the blood pumping through his chest. Chase could hear her calling his sister's name, but that awful silence greeted her.

Where in the world would the girl have gone, and how would they find her? He rechecked her room to ensure he hadn't missed a note or some other clue about her whereabouts.

Finding nothing, he maneuvered himself down the steps as quickly as possible. Madison was at the counter, studying her phone.

"Did she text you? Do we call the cops right away? Do you have that Brody kid's number? Where else would she have gone?"

His chest clenched as Madison gasped, then raised her gaze to his. "I have location services turned on for her phone. She's in Montrose," she said like she couldn't quite believe her own words.

"Where?" The name sounded vaguely familiar, but his panicked brain couldn't process the specific location.

"It's over twenty miles away. I don't know what she'd be doing there or how she would have…"

Her eyes widened. "There's a bus station in Montrose," she said, sounding as panicked as Chase felt.

"Grab the keys," Chase told her. "I'll get my phone, and we can call the authorities on our way. We'll stop her from whatever she has planned next."

They had to.

Chapter Twelve

Starlight and Montrose were only twenty miles away but driving the mountain roads at night had made the journey feel interminably long.

On the way, Madison had called Nick Dunlap, Starlight's police chief. He'd contacted his counterpart in Montrose, who'd agreed to pick up the girl from the bus station, so at least they knew she was safe.

There had been many things Madison wanted to say to Chase, advice she had for how he might talk to his stepsister. But after how he'd spoken to her earlier, she didn't think he'd want her input. She understood it wasn't her place to give it, even if she believed in her heart it would help.

"I owe you an apology," he finally said into the

weighted silence between them. "Both you and Stella. That's why I was coming upstairs, but I can't even put words together now. I'm angry and terrified and guilty, and it's too much."

"You'll figure it out," she told him because it was also all she had to offer. "We'll talk later. Right now, let's concentrate on getting Stella home."

Chase nodded and returned his gaze to the inky forest surrounding them. The darkness could swallow a person whole if they weren't careful. Stella and Chase were not being careful with each other. Another thing Madison was an expert on, but she kept that to herself as well.

Madison followed Chase into the local police station when they finally arrived in Montrose. Stella sat on a bench in the lobby, her arms wrapped tight around the backpack she held in her lap.

Madison didn't miss the flash of relief in the girl's tired gaze before she shuttered her features.

Her jaw jutted out in a defiant tilt. Her chin wobbled the tiniest bit, giving away her feelings.

Madison wasn't sure what Chase noticed, but she swallowed back tears as he went to stand in front of Stella.

He pried her arms from around the backpack, lifted her onto her feet and pulled her into a tight hug.

"I'm sorry. I'm sorry I made you feel like you had no other choice but to run away. I'm sorry for more than I can even tell you, Stel."

There was a beat of silence during which Madison held her breath, wondering how the girl would respond. Praying that her response would open the door to forgiveness on both their parts.

It was a big step for Madison, who wasn't usually the praying type. Maybe it worked or maybe Stella was just as smart as Madi believed her to be, because she sobbed out an apology.

"I'm sorry I ran away and let my dumb friends into your studio. I should have told you right away. I'm so sorry you almost died, Chase. I don't want you to die."

He pulled back and looked down into his sister's blotchy face. "That might be the nicest thing anyone's ever said to me."

Madison felt like she'd won the lottery as Stella smiled in response to her brother's teasing.

A law enforcement officer appeared from the back of the station. "You're a lucky young lady," he told Stella, then turned to Chase. "She hitchhiked here, planning to catch a bus to Seattle."

The knot of tension in Chase's jaw was evident, but he held it together as he released Stella. "I hope you learned a lesson."

"I have," she promised. "I'm sorry for leaving and for scaring you. I'm sure you're sick of dealing with my problems."

"There will be consequences," he answered calmly, "but the important thing is that you are safe. You're what matters most."

Madison was so proud of him at that moment, and her heart thumped wildly. She thought back to days after she ran away from the temporary home where she and her sister had been placed. Although she'd believed she was making the right decision to ensure Jenna's future, she'd also wanted somebody—anybody—to come after her. She'd desperately wanted a reason to believe everything would be okay, not just for her sister but for herself as well.

If only there had been someone who'd seen past the troubled, angry teenager to the sad, scared kid who yearned to feel safe and protected. How many times had she wished for a different fate?

She'd figured out how to take care of herself until she let her demons run the show. But beneath the brash, independent exterior the rest of the world saw was the abandoned waif she'd never left behind.

Would she ever be able to let go of that girl?

She suddenly realized that was part of what motivated her to help Stella. If she made a difference to this kid who reminded her of herself, could she finally overcome the memories and regret that still haunted her?

The police officer asked to speak with Chase alone, and Chase led Stella toward Madison. He trusted her with his sister, which had to count for something. The teenager followed her out into the cold.

"I'm sorry that you have to be involved in all of this," Stella told her. "I'm sure you regret helping—"

"I'm going to stop you right there. No more apologies."

The girl blinked. "But I *am* sorry."

"Your words are starting to feel empty," Madison told her. "I'm not passing judgment. I've made more than my share of empty promises to people, but they don't do any good. You've had a rough time, but you've also made serious mistakes. I can't imagine what it's like to lose parents who loved you. It was hard enough to lose a second-rate mom. But I believe your mom and dad are watching over you, Stella. You have guardian angels going to bat for you, and they've helped you come through what you have unscathed."

"I don't believe in angels." The girl's expression turned mulish even as tears filled her eyes.

"You should, because it's important to honor being on the receiving end of miracles the way you have been. That faith is what gets you through. Nobody can bring back your mom and dad, but you know they loved you. You know they wanted a good life for you. And I know—" Madison lifted a finger and pointed at the girl "—that your parents had expectations of you. That's what good parents do. You might think you can flout the rules and get away with it. You flaunt your orphan girl status with boys and adults, but it's not going to make your heart hurt any less. Trust me."

Stella kicked at the worn asphalt of the parking lot with the toe of her battered sneaker. A gust of wind whipped past them, almost as sharp as Madison's words.

She figured it was past time for a little tough love when it came to Stella. If Chase was going to be softer, she could point out some hard truths. They were for the girl's benefit, but it was a balance.

She still wanted Stella to know that she was loved and that mistakes didn't define her. So she reached out and grabbed the girl in a stiff hug. "You're going to be okay, even if I have to fight tooth and nail to make sure of it. I don't regret bringing you here, Stella. You or your brother. And that's new, because regret is one of my go-to emotions."

"I'm going to do better," the girl said softly.

"I know," Madison agreed, then released Stella when a shiver rippled through the girl. She opened the back door of the SUV. "Let's go home."

It took about twenty minutes for Chase to return to the car. He didn't say much about his conversation with the police officer.

Neither he nor Madison said much because Stella fell asleep almost as soon as they pulled out of the police station parking lot. When they arrived back at her house, the girl woke up and followed them inside.

She stopped at the foot of the stairs. "I'm not going to run away again," she said to her brother. "I don't like having to apologize to you."

"Whatever works," he told her with a grin, then turned as Madison approached him.

"You did good tonight," she said. "I know it couldn't have been easy, but I think it made a real difference with her."

"I hope so, because I'm not sure how much more I can take. Thank you for being here for both of us. I don't know what you said to her out in the parking lot, but I think it also made a difference."

She offered him a soft smile. "Whatever works. Now you should get to bed, too."

"Stay with me." He cupped her face in his hands and dropped a kiss on her forehead. "I have no right to ask, but I need you tonight."

She nodded as her throat went dry. When was the last time someone had needed her in that way?

She would have told anyone who asked that she didn't want to be needed. But Chase's words filled her heart.

She cocked her head as she heard a faint noise come from somewhere in the house. "Did you hear that?"

He frowned. "I didn't hear anything."

"It sounded like bells ringing." She thought of the Christmas movie that was her sister's favorite, the one they'd watched year after year because it was free on television during the holidays. She thought about the conversations she'd had with Stella.

"An angel got their wings tonight," she whispered.

The next morning Madison left the house before the sun came up while both Chase and Stella were still asleep. She turned off the Trophy Room alarm, entered the kitchen and then got to work.

She needed time by herself to reset, regroup and shore up the defenses she thought were solid around her heart.

Chase and Stella had wormed their way through them with seemingly little trouble or outright effort. What was it about the two of them that made her heart insist it had found the family she'd never thought she wanted?

She'd known them for less than a month—maybe she'd been acquainted with Stella for longer at the community center—but now she'd quickly grown to love the girl.

The word should have felt bitter on her tongue, but it filled her with a satisfaction she didn't realize she craved.

In truth, Madison hadn't known she was capable of caring for people the way she did Chase and his sister. Spending the night with him holding her… well, it scared her to her bones. It frightened her to need someone, let alone a man who professed that he didn't have a heart. She knew that wasn't the case but was also aware of the lengths people would go to prove themselves right. Even if it meant hurting those around them in the process.

She'd done that often enough, especially when she'd been drinking. She was placing uncooked lasagna noodles in the boiling pot of water when she heard voices from the front of the restaurant. A moment later, Tessa, Cory and Ella entered the kitchen.

"Are you still tracking me?" she demanded, pointing a finger at Ella. "I thought you were going to turn it off."

"Jordan got a notification when the alarm was deactivated this morning," Cory explained. "We figured it was you. It's time for an intervention."

"Exactly," Tessa said, nodding. "Where have you been?"

"Where have *I* been?" Madison lifted a brow.

"Yes, you missed cooking club recently, and you're the only one of us who likes to cook."

"Does it matter?" Madison didn't bother to keep the bitterness from her voice. "At least one of you has canceled every month since this summer. I figured it wasn't a priority to you. Why should it be to me?" She adjusted the heat on the stove. "I know you've got these great loves now, so you don't need cooking club. For me, that's not the case."

Cory frowned. "I love this group, but I've been busy with the jewelry business taking off and the baby, but that doesn't mean I don't care."

"We all care," Tessa added.

"Stop." Madison whirled to face her friends. "I'm not complaining. I know you're all busy and have important stuff going on. I have stuff, too, you know."

"Is that the reason you're here this early?" Cory asked.

"I'm cooking for your community Christmas supper. Since Chase and Stella have been here, I haven't been able to do my weekly shifts at the youth center in Seattle. I figured I could pitch in closer to home."

She felt a blush color her cheeks as her friends stared at her. "No need to look shocked. I've been volunteering for my sister for a while. This isn't so different."

"That was your sister," Ella said. "We thought…"

Her friends looked at each other.

"What? You thought I volunteered out of guilt?"

The three of them appeared equally abashed. Madison laughed. "You're right—or at least, you're not wrong. It started as guilt with Jenna. I wanted to make up for what I'd done to her—as if that were possible. I like cooking for people, and not just when I'm getting paid."

She waved a lasagna noodle at them. "You three moochers are another example of that, although maybe not as worthy as the kids in my sister's program or the people Jordan plans to feed on Christmas Eve."

"Do you want some help?" Cory asked. "I haven't been around much, but I'm here now."

"I am, too. I can help," Tessa offered.

"I need coffee." Ella yawned. "Tell me there's a coffeepot in this kitchen."

"It's behind the bar," Madison told her.

"I'll help you get a pot brewing," Cory said. Then the two of them disappeared into the bar area.

"Nobody was trying to ghost you," Tessa said. "But

you're right. We've all been caught up in our own lives. The Chop It Like It's Hot cooking club is a priority. Our friendship is a priority."

"I know." Madison appreciated hearing the words just the same. "Grab a couple of eggs out of the fridge, and we'll start on the cheese sauce."

"As we work, can we talk about Chase Kent?"

"I prefer not to."

"I know. That's why I want to talk. He reminds me of you."

Madison snorted. "He's hard on himself. He wants people to believe he's the guy who doesn't care. He cares about his sister."

Madison came to stand next to Tessa as her friend removed the egg carton from the refrigerator. Madison reached for the cheese. She used three different varieties in her lasagna.

When she'd first started volunteering for her sister's program, one of the other adults involved had told her that she could skimp on ingredients. Even if she made food without her usual attention to detail or cheaper cuts of meat or less cheese than the recipe called for, the kids wouldn't notice or care since they were so used to far less.

Madison had bought the most expensive steak she could find for her next shift. Her appreciation of food and quality ingredients had inspired her throughout her career. It wasn't as if she expected to offer that sort of inspiration to someone else, but she would never skimp. Everyone deserved good food.

When she was teaching classes, she was cognizant of the financial status of her students and certainly knew how to make tasty dishes from ingredients that didn't break the bank.

But this was a special dinner for her friends and neighbors. She might not have the gift of making people feel at ease like Jordan and Cory did when they sponsored these community meals, but she could feed people.

She had something to offer.

"He cares a lot," Tessa said, bringing Madison's attention back to the present. "Yes, he loves his sister, who's an absolute sweetheart. She might be his biggest priority. But he's good with the other kids, too. Especially the squirrelly boys. He did this exercise with them the other day where he gave out pastels and had all the kids close their eyes and draw based on what the music made them feel when Helen played it at the piano."

Tessa closed her eyes as if she were picturing the scene. "He told them that when they were singing, they should channel those feelings because the audience would feel the music through their voices. I don't know if some of the little kids got it, although they had fun coloring. But he made a difference to the older ones. I think Stella is proud that her brother is a famous artist. Most kids around here have gone to Seattle on a field trip and seen some of his work in public parks and museums. Somebody told me he donates all of that."

"He's a good guy," Madison agreed. "You don't have to convince me."

"I'm suggesting he might be the right guy for you."

"Nope."

"Madison, come on. I've seen the way you look at each other."

"I will ban you from my kitchen."

"I'm helping."

"You're irritating me." She glanced at the door to the front of the bar. "Please, Tessa. I don't want the third degree from Ella and Cory. It's…" She shrugged. "It's a lot."

"Oh, honey." Tessa gave her a quick hug. "Love is always a lot, but it's worth it."

"I didn't say anything about love."

Tessa squeezed again. "You didn't have to. It's written all over your face."

Madison made a mental note to work on fixing her face.

Chapter Thirteen

Chase stared at the doctor who stood before him during his follow-up visit two days later.

"What do you mean another surgery?" he demanded.

The orthopedic surgeon Chase had been seeing in Starlight rubbed two fingers on his forehead. "We knew this was a possibility. Unfortunately, the tendons aren't healing the way we expected them to."

"I thought my leg *was* healing. You cleared me to use a cane instead of crutches. I can put weight on it. I'm supposed to start driving soon. Most importantly, I need to get back into my studio so I can rebuild."

"You have improved. It's remarkable," the doctor told him with a smile that Chase wanted to rip off

MICHELLE MAJOR   171

the man's face. "I didn't handle the initial surgery,
and you are welcome to revisit the doctor in Seattle
for a second opinion. However, my recommendation
is another procedure. The recovery won't be as long
or involved as the first one, but—"

"It will keep me from getting back to normal life
for how long?"

"At least one additional month," the man answered. Chase guessed that the doctor was around
his age. Handsome, fit and annoyingly empathetic.
"Hopefully not longer, especially if you keep up with
PT and exercise independently."

Chase's gut clenched. He hadn't expected this news.
It was a blow. He thought his time being dependent
would come to an end after Christmas.

Even though the life he'd had in Seattle held little
appeal compared to his time in Starlight, returning
to it was a given.

He needed a routine. He needed his independence
because he'd gotten too comfortable in this small
town with Madison in his life.

They couldn't last. He wasn't good for her. He
wasn't good for anyone in his current shape.

Chase would lose his mind in another three to
four weeks. He was going to lose Madison, of course.
Stella would go back to school and he would go back
to his studio because it was easier to be alone there.

He could hire somebody to help around the house
and a driver for his sister, but he didn't want to do it

alone. He'd come to rely on Madison—not just for meals or teenage-parenting advice.

"You should talk to your doctor in the city if he's the one you want doing the surgery." The Starlight surgeon, Marcus Wiley, flipped through Chase's chart.

"You're trying to get rid of me already, Doc?" Chase tried for humor, but the words came out on a bitter exhalation.

"I'm happy to continue treating you," Dr. Wiley told him. "But if I do, I'd like you to commit to staying in Starlight for the duration of your recovery. I don't like to lose touch with my patients."

"I appreciate everything you've done, Doc, but I can't commit to being in Starlight beyond the holidays. Having a follow-up surgery in Seattle is the best option for everyone." The words felt like spikes on his tongue, but he had to say them.

"You're staying with Madison Maurer right now, correct?"

"Yes." It was a small town, but Chase wasn't sure how the doctor knew or why it was important. "She's a friend of my sister's and agreed to let us stay with her over winter break."

"Right." Something flashed in the doctor's arresting blue eyes that looked like a mix of hope and relief.

Strange.

"I met Madison through Ella. She's a fascinating person."

"To say the least," Chase murmured.

"So the two of you aren't…" The doctor raised an eyebrow. "A couple?"

Chase thought about falling asleep with Madison next to him, the way she snored softly and fidgeted in her sleep, curling her body into his. "We aren't a couple."

"Any chance you're willing to do me a solid and put in a good word?"

Bum leg be damned, Chase wanted to kick the absolute piss out of this guy. First, the doctor gave him the devastating news about another surgery. Now he wanted help asking out Madison.

Oh, hell no.

"Sure. Give me your phone, and I'll put in her number."

"Great. I've been looking for an excuse to reach out."

"You can tell her I suggested it." It felt as though Chase was shoving toothpicks under his nail beds. He smiled at the doctor. "She's a lot of fun and deserves somebody great."

"Thanks," the man said. "We'll make sure to get your film to the office in Seattle, and I'll reach out to the doctor. I know this isn't what you wanted or expected to hear, but you're still lucky. Even if the road to recovery isn't a straight line, you will get there. You've got people to take care of you. That's important."

What was important was that Chase not be any more of a burden to Madison and Stella. The two people who'd already gone above and beyond for him.

He didn't want to depend on anyone. It had been one thing to come to Starlight after the initial accident when he'd been so out of it. That was for Stella's benefit. Anything more was selfish.

Chase knew what happened when he allowed himself to need or depend on someone. They left. He had to cut ties before that happened.

He needed to walk away so that no one had the opportunity to leave him behind.

"Thanks, Doc," he said as he typed Madison's contact information into Marcus Wiley's phone. "Have a merry Christmas."

"You, too. Maybe the New Year will be a perfect time for me to get to know your friend better. I appreciate you putting in a good word."

"No problem." Chase ignored the pit in his belly. "None at all."

He walked out of the medical center and climbed into the back of the car he'd paid to wait during his appointment. He hadn't told Madison or Stella he was going to see Dr. Wiley today. Chase had mistakenly believed he'd be receiving good news from the doctor today based on how things had been progressing.

He knew setbacks were normal, given the severity of his accident. It didn't offer solace. He was a man who had structured his life to adhere to a plan.

Nothing was going according to plan in Starlight.

The house was empty when he returned. Another reason he hadn't shared his appointment was because Madison had made plans to take Stella to Spokane for Christmas shopping.

They'd invited him, but he figured his sister would have a better time if he wasn't there.

Now he wished he'd skipped the appointment. Ignorance was bliss.

He walked into the house and limped to his bedroom using his new cane. Another surgery and another month. He knew what would come after that. His cousin had left another message the night Stella had run away. Familiar irritation at the unfairness of life consumed him.

He stumbled as the cane hooked on the edge of the carpet. Curses flew from his mouth, and he tossed the stupid stick across the room. It banged into the dresser, and the box of oil pastels sitting there unused spilled onto the floor.

He'd brought some of the art supplies he'd had in the Seattle house with him but hadn't been able to get himself to create anything new. Not when he couldn't function on his terms.

As he hobbled over to retrieve the small sticks, the colors and patterns they made on the floor had his breath catching. Images exploded in his head. It was the way things often started with him—a feeling, just like he'd said to the kids about the music. He quickly grabbed the pad of paper he'd shoved in the closet and sat on the floor to begin sketching.

A design appeared from deep in his subconscious. Emotion pricked the backs of his eyes. The thing he hadn't said out loud or even admitted to himself was that he'd been afraid the accident had robbed him of his creativity.

He'd never given much thought to the muse, because ideas flowed easily, until they hadn't. It had been easy enough to pretend like he wasn't creating because of his recovery and the fact he didn't have access to his studio.

But he didn't need a studio, because everything he needed to make art was inside himself.

"Chase."

He didn't look up at his name being called in Madison's feminine voice. How much time had passed since he'd started drawing?

"Wow, you've been busy," she said a moment later.

He finally paused, blinking as he returned to himself and glanced around at the papers surrounding him. There were pictures of waves and colors and shapes. His glass sculptures often started with sketches. But these felt different. They weren't just the potential inspiration for something he would create out of glass.

They were creative expressions on their own,

something he could do even without being able to hold the heavy iron in the fire. It wasn't as though without his physicality he had no options for creativity, although he'd wondered if the artistic life as he knew it might be over if he couldn't do the thing he knew so well and that had brought him fame and fortune.

Drawing was how his love of art had started, but it had been years since he'd had the urge to for its own sake.

"I'm drawing," he said, embarrassed as he realized how stupid that sounded since it was obvious.

If she noticed, Madison didn't comment. She simply walked toward him and lowered herself to the trunk at the end of the bed.

"What brought on this flurry of creativity?"

He shrugged. "That's like asking what brings on a sudden tsunami. It comes from deep inside me. I can't stop. I wouldn't want to, if I'm being honest. It's precious." He started to gather the scattered papers. "Is Stella here?"

Madison nodded. "She went to her room to hide your present."

"She didn't need to buy me anything."

"I know," she said with a secret smile. "But you'll like what she chose. She's also getting ready, so we can go to caroling in town tonight. Remember? All of us are caroling."

Chase gave a mock shudder. "I can't believe I agreed to go. Let's pretend I didn't."

"No chance. You're not leaving me alone in this. I can't even carry a tune." She bent to lift one of the drawings, inadvertently revealing the top of her breast as the collar of her sweater gaped. "These are beautiful. Are they similar to what you've done in the past?"

"No. They're different than the sketches I use as a basis for the glass pieces, more like how I used to draw when I was a kid. I stopped because my dad told me girls and sissies do art. Then he handed me a football."

"It's hard for me to reconcile that the father you had is the same one Stella talks about."

Chase tried to laugh it off. "I was a starter kid and a colossal failure. At least he figured out how to do better with her."

"Which doesn't make it any better for you."

"Maybe not, but I wouldn't wish the dad I had on Stella. Not for a second."

"That's big of you."

"Oh, I'm big," he agreed with a wink. "As you know." He felt a grin split his face as her cheeks bloomed with color.

"You have a healthy opinion of yourself," she said, rolling her eyes. "Also, you're not wrong."

"Come over here." He crooked a finger.

"You're dirty," she said but lowered herself from

the trunk to the carpet. She sat on her knees, her jeans brushing his.

The touch was so featherlight there was no explanation for its impact. Heat radiated through him, and he reached out to touch her cheek, leaving a smudge of yellow chalk on her soft skin.

"Now you're dirty, too. Kiss me, Madison."

"I will if you promise not to put your grubby artist paws on me before we head into town."

"That's a hard bargain," he said like he was genuinely struggling with her request. "Because I want to touch you. I want to make a mess of you from head to toe."

"Later," she promised with a small secret smile.

Chase had pretty much worked through his anger after the news from the doctor. If he hadn't, then kissing Madison would have accomplished anything his creative release hadn't. As their mouths melded, he realized the flavor of vanilla would be forever associated with this woman.

Her mouth was soft and giving under his. A part of him wanted to tell her about his news from the doctor. He wondered if she would invite him to stay. What if instead of rebuilding his studio in Seattle, he made Starlight his home? The thought was both exhilarating and terrifying.

She pulled back suddenly. "Am I boring you?"

He blinked. "Of course not."

"You stopped kissing me right in the middle of kissing me."

"I was thinking."

"First, you need to work on your multitasking, and second, what were you thinking?"

"About us." He answered honestly, wondering exactly how much he should reveal. What if he shared too much and scared her away?

"It must have been a deep thought."

Madison plopped back on the trunk at the sound of footsteps thundering down the staircase.

A moment later, Stella appeared in the doorway. "What's going on?" Her gaze darted between them. "What are you two doing?"

"I'm drawing," Chase said and cleared his throat when the words came out gruffer than he'd meant. "I've been drawing this afternoon. How was shopping?"

"Spokane was awesome. I got you something."

"It better be good," he told her with an exaggerated wink, then immediately shook his head. "That was a joke. It's nice that you thought of me. I don't care if you got me a rock paperweight. It's the thought that counts."

"It's good." She offered an almost shy smile, then looked more closely at the papers on the floor. The excitement in her tone humbled him.

He'd done nothing to deserve these two people caring about him, and yet they did anyway. His chest ached because their kindness would make it that much harder when it was time to say goodbye.

If only he believed he could be brave enough to attempt to claim the happiness Madison and Stella offered.

Chapter Fourteen

Madison smiled at the compliment one of the older women in the caroling group gave her about her empanada recipe and promised she would share the details. Certain chefs refused to give away the secrets of their best recipes, but she'd always believed the more people who enjoyed them, the better.

There was no higher compliment than someone asking for a recipe, and she didn't believe it would impact her business. First, everything she made was delicious enough to bring customers through the door. Second, going out to dinner wasn't just about the food, although it made a big difference. Sharing the experience with friends and family was just as important.

Sort of like tonight's caroling experience. The group had toured the neighborhoods surrounding downtown Starlight, and although Madison mainly had mouthed the words—the fact that she couldn't carry a tune out of a bucket had been no joke—she loved every minute of it.

If she weren't careful, this holiday season might turn her into one of those annoying people who looked forward to Christmas all year round. The season had started with the sole purpose of helping Stella and Chase, but she was getting just as much out of it as—if not more than—the two of them.

For years, she'd associated the holidays with reminders of what her life lacked. Traditions that hadn't been a part of her childhood seemed to be the foundation of memories for other people. Slowly, she was coming to see that she and her sister had made their own memories and traditions, even though they weren't perfect or cookie-cutter.

There had even been a couple of times throughout the years when their mom had been in a good place at this time of the year. Madison had forced herself to forget those times because opening her heart would elicit too high a price when things came crashing down.

But she was different now, not a little girl with other people in charge. She called the shots, so she was responsible for her own happiness.

Life in Starlight made her happy. Chase and Stella

made her happy, too. If she couldn't stop from falling for him, at least she would have the comfort of knowing she'd made a difference in his life after he left. He was even creating again. From personal experience, Madison knew that was a massive step in the right direction.

Stella called her name as she ran up and grabbed Madison's arms. "Brody and some of his friends are going to the coffee shop for hot chocolate. Can I go? He said his mom will give me a ride home later."

"What did your brother say?" Madison glanced around for Chase and saw him in conversation with Josh and his brother, Parker. Her heart seemed to skip a beat as he looked up and met her gaze with a subtle nod.

"He said it was okay but to ask you."

The older woman next to her chuckled. "The man always makes sure the buck stops with Mom." Madison's gaze darted to Stella just in time to see the flash of pain in the girl's clear gray eyes. She wasn't the girl's mom or anywhere close, and they both knew it. But there was no point in making the moment any more awkward.

"Sure, that's great. Have fun." Her voice sounded ridiculously chipper to her own ears. "No caffeine, though," she added, "or you'll be up all night."

Oh, Lord. Now she really did sound like somebody's mom, even though she had no right. Stella

took it in stride and nodded. Somehow Madison
knew she'd said the right thing.

"I'll see you later. Decaf only." Stella turned and
hurried toward a group of teenagers gathered at the
edge of the small crowd.

"Cute girl," the older woman said with an indul-
gent smile. "She looks like you."

Madison gasped like she'd taken an emotional
right hook straight to the solar plexus.

"She's not…" Before Madison could explain, the
woman turned away.

"That was fun," Tessa said as she approached. Her
face fell as she took in Madison's expression. "What
happened? What's wrong? Are you okay?"

"Somebody thought I was Stella's mother."

Tessa let out a stifled laugh. "That must be a first
for you."

"You have no idea. It's like pointing to a cobra or
tiger or some animal that eats its babies and handing them a mom-of-the-year trophy."

"You sell yourself short too often," her friend said,
giving Madison a comforting pat.

"You've been accused of being temperamental, but
I don't think anybody's suggested cannibalism. You're
young to have a teenage daughter. That's what I was
hinting at."

"It's more," Madison insisted. "Because I'm less.
You know what I mean."

"I do, but you should start seeing yourself the way

other people view you. The way Stella sees you. A girl could do a lot worse than having someone like you as a mother."

"She could also do a lot better." Madison felt her eyes go wide. "Did I miss the boat? Should I have been helping Chase find a girlfriend while he was here? If he were in a relationship, it would be easier to take on the parental responsibilities. A woman could help soften him."

"Isn't that what you're doing?"

"I'm more along the lines of respite care. You know, somebody who can handle something for the short term. I've never been anybody's long-term bet."

Tessa shook her head. "You don't know that because you've never opened yourself up to the possibility," her friend countered, then was drawn away by Carson's daughter.

Madison understood the dread of being unable to keep her sister and herself safe from random creeps their mother brought home when they were kids.

The bone-deep fear of struggling to remove her sister from the car to safety the night of the accident. But nothing in her life and the many mistakes she'd made prepared her for the pure terror of *wanting*.

Wanting to believe in possibilities. Wanting to say yes to the future and everything it might include.

What if she wasn't the person she'd always believed—the one who brought pain and trouble into the lives of people she cared about?

After so long and so many mistakes, maybe she'd shrugged off the heavy mantle of her destructive tendencies. She might not only be capable of giving love but worthy of receiving it in return. What if she could attain a happy ending? What would she risk to make those possibilities a reality?

The idea of it had her trembling all over. She searched the crowd to find Chase, realizing he was critical to that future. Understanding that she needed him to be willing to take the same risk. She turned at her name spoken in an unfamiliar male voice.

"Hi," a handsome man said as he smiled at her. He wore a gray wool jacket with a camel-colored sweater peeking out from the collar, dark jeans and leather boots that seemed expensive. "I'm Marcus Wiley. We met at a barbecue at Ella and Josh's a few months ago."

Madison's thoughts were so disjointed that it took her a minute to register the face of the man standing in front of her. "I remember you. You're a doctor. You're Chase's doctor."

"Has he mentioned me to you?" The man sounded strangely hopeful.

"Yeah, I think he did," she said. "A couple of times."

The doctor blew out a breath. "That's great."

"I know you didn't do the initial surgery, but it's good of you to help him while he's in town."

"Sure," Marcus said, running a hand through his wavy blond hair.

Madison remembered Ella telling their group of friends at cooking club that half the nurses in the Starlight hospital, both married and single, were in love with Dr. Wiley. Madison understood why. The man was tall and broad-shouldered with a movie star cleft in his chin, but his eyes were kind.

He might send pulses racing in the hospital halls but didn't do it for Madison. He was a little too earnest and classically good-looking for her.

As a kid, she'd always loved Lemonhead candies. They were one of the few things she could scrape enough change together to afford at the convenience store around the corner from the cramped, crummy apartment where they lived.

Even if she'd had more money, she wouldn't have chosen a regular chocolate bar, even the kind with nuts. She liked how the lemon candy started with a bit of sugar and then made her pucker from the sour.

Madison appreciated suffering through a few seconds of uncomfortable tartness before the reward of the sugary center. She preferred a man who was like that candy, where she had to work to find the gooey heart of them.

A man like Chase.

"I appreciated when he said he'd put in a good word for me," Marcus told her. "To be honest, I've wanted to ask you out since we met that day at Josh's."

Madison blinked. "Ask me out," she repeated. Her distracted brain quickly regained its focus. "Chase told you to ask me out?"

Marcus offered a self-deprecating grin. "It was my idea. Chase confirmed it was a good one. I was going to wait until after the New Year. I'm sure you're busy with the holiday crowd coming to the bar, plus having houseguests. The hospital's a zoo right now. I'd hoped we could go out once things quieted down?"

"On a date," she blurted.

He nodded, brows furrowed. "That was the idea. Chase said you weren't seeing anyone."

Her mouth went dry. She bit down on the inside of her cheek to keep from letting out a disappointed whimper.

Chase wanted to set her up with another man. Of course he did. His time with Madison didn't mean anything. They were together because they lived in the same house at the moment—two consenting adults scratching an itch.

She was easy.

Her breath caught in her throat. Her mother had been easy, and it was the one thing Madison had vowed not to take after.

"Let me give you my number," she told Marcus,

still unaffected by his kind eyes and thousand-watt smile. She'd gone cold on the inside.

"Chase already did." Marcus laughed and looked down at the ground before meeting her gaze again. Adorable. He was literally adorable and totally unsuitable for her, but he apparently didn't realize that.

"He gave you my number," she murmured.

"I hope that's okay."

"Of course. And you're right. I'm busy these days, but let's make a plan if you want to. Busy shouldn't stop us."

"I'll make time around your schedule."

Emotion clogged Madison's throat. A handsome, kind surgeon wanted to make time for her, and she was hung up on a tortured jerk of an artist who could sleep with her one night and then...

"I'm curious—how long ago did Chase give you my number?"

"When I saw him in my office earlier. Like I told you, I've been meaning to reach out. I'm glad I finally got a chance to talk to you."

So Chase had been ready to set her up with another man shortly after they'd been together. Good to know.

"I normally don't go into work until close to eleven," she said. "Sometimes earlier if I have extra prep, but there's more flexibility in the morning. What do you think about a coffee date next week?"

Her heart threw itself against her rib cage like some kind of warning. It couldn't end well with Marcus Wiley when Madison's desire to go out with him was mostly founded in bitterness.

"How about Wednesday?"

"That's great." He pulled a phone out of his back pocket. "Oh, wait. It's Christmas Eve. You probably—"

"It's fine with me, unless you have plans. You aren't seeing family?"

He shrugged. "I'm driving to my parents' house in Portland on Christmas morning after one last overnight shift. It would certainly start the holiday off right to spend it with you."

She nodded. "Let's meet at Main Street Perk at eight."

He flashed a smile that was toothpaste-commercial bright. "I look forward to it."

Heart still pounding, she turned away and started walking toward the alley between the building that housed Trophy Room and the realty office next door.

"That was more fun than I expected," Chase said as he broke off from the group he was standing with and moved toward her.

Madison hadn't realized he was so close or she would have headed in the other direction.

"Thanks for forcing me to participate."

"I didn't force you to do anything," she said. "I don't have any hold or claim on you. You are simply

Stella's brother, and I'm helping your sister. I like your sister."

He gave her a quizzical look. "Did somebody step on your foot while we were caroling?"

"No."

They were at the entrance of the alley now. A light in the center cast a warm glow, but Madison felt anything but warm. She crossed her arms over the puffer coat she wore when the chilled air seemed to seep into her bones.

"Did you not have fun?"

"I had a lovely time. In fact, I spoke with a friend of yours tonight. Dr. Marcus Wiley."

"What did he tell you?"

"Something along the lines of you thinking he and I would make a cute couple."

A muscle jumped in Chase's jaw as he glanced past her like it was too difficult to meet her gaze. "He's a good man. Decent. Well respected."

"Then why on earth would you think I was right for him?" She turned and strode down the alley, aware of the thump of his cane as he followed.

"He likes you," Chase said.

She turned on him and forced herself to stand her ground when he crowded her. "I thought *you* liked me," she said quietly, then immediately regretted the words and what they revealed.

He reached up and rubbed a thumb over her

cheek. "I do, Madison. More than is smart for either of us."

A Christmas song played in the distance, and she breathed out a laugh despite her anger.

Understanding dawned in Chase's eyes. "Whamageddon. We've been hit." His mouth ticked up at one side.

Madison wanted to offer a denial, not that they'd heard the Christmas song and the silly game was over, but that they'd gone down together.

"Last Christmas, I gave you my heart. The very next day, you gave it away."

She didn't want to share even this tiny connection. When it came to Chase, the devil really was in the details. The small moments had her falling for him, and he had just proved that was a terrible idea.

"I guess the game is over," she said matter-of-factly. "I'm going to check on the meat I have marinating for tomorrow's special. I can give you the key and meet you at the car." The errand wasn't necessary, but she needed a few moments to collect herself, to quickly rebuild the wall around her heart.

To remind herself that she couldn't let Chase chip away at it again.

"I'll tag along," he said. "It's late."

"It's Starlight," she argued but headed toward the back of the building again.

"Are you going out with Marcus?" Chase's tone seemed almost aggressively emotionless.

"Yes. Next week."

"Before Christmas?"

"Is that a problem?" she asked as they rounded the corner.

"No. I just thought…"

"You gave him my number, Chase. Not long after we were together. You made things clear."

"I didn't mean—"

"Stop." She placed a hand on his forearm. "Do you hear that?"

He tipped his head to one side. "It sounds like crying."

"An animal in distress." Madison glanced up and down the alley, which was empty of both cars and people. Starlight rolled up the sidewalks early during the week.

"There." Chase pointed toward the bar's rear entrance, the door that led to Madison's kitchen.

A cardboard box sat on the steps and seemed to be jiggling. She moved forward.

"Be careful," Chase warned behind her. "It could be a wild animal."

The tiny mewing coming from the box didn't sound wild. It was sad and weak.

She bent over and opened the box, then muttered a curse. "Kittens," she announced as Chase came to stand next to her.

Two shivering balls of fluff. The kittens were mostly black, but each had a bit of white on their faces, and both had four white paws. They had long whiskers and were shivering in the cold, gray eyes slowly blinking up at her.

"Who would leave kittens on a doorstep in this cold?"

Madison's heart stuttered. "What if I hadn't wanted to stop in the kitchen? Sophie and Miles have gone home. They might have been out here overnight." She picked up one of the tiny creatures and tucked it under her chin. The little animal burrowed closer like it craved her heat.

"It's supposed to snow overnight." Almost immediately, a few fluffy flakes appeared from the black sky. She placed the kitten back in the box before picking it up. "The beef will have to wait until tomorrow. I need to get these two warmed up."

"We," Chase corrected. "I'm here to help. Is there a shelter in town?"

"Yes, but it's not open this late. The closest emergency vet is an hour away. I'll take them home and then call—"

"Maybe one of your friends would be willing to keep them?"

Madison stopped and hugged the box closer to her chest. "Are you insinuating I'm not equipped to handle these kittens?"

"They're babies, Madison, and clearly in distress. They need somebody—"

"Maternal?" she suggested.

He made that familiar growling sound, and her body reacted in spite of her heart.

"Somebody with experience," he clarified.

"I can keep them alive overnight. I have a way with injured creatures. After all, I haven't killed you yet."

"I wasn't trying to offend you."

"It comes naturally. Good to know." She moved past him, and he wisely didn't say anything more.

They made their way to her vehicle, and she placed the box on his lap after he got in and buckled his seat belt. "Is this too much responsibility for you, Chase? Because I can put them in the back seat."

He shook his head, not rising to her bait. "It's fine."

She climbed into the driver's side and cranked the heat, but it didn't truly warm up for several minutes. By then, she had tracked down the number of the local vet and received detailed instructions on what to do for the kittens.

She stopped at the local grocery to buy a couple of cans of food. When they got to the house, she took the box from Chase and headed inside. Now that she had the tiny creatures at her home, panic seized Madison's chest. Chase had been right, of course. She should have called Tessa or Cory or even Ella, who was a nurse.

There were a whole host of people who would

know more about how to care for abandoned kittens than her. But she was committed now, and to her surprise, so was Chase.

He gathered blankets and the heating pad from her linen closet, and they set up an area in Madison's small laundry room.

To her delight, the kittens almost immediately toddled over to the water dish and then eagerly lapped up the food she offered. One of them was quiet, but the other squeaked out its pleasure. Although the kittens were clearly underweight, they weren't as small as they'd looked in the box. It gave her hope that they'd be okay.

"I forgot a litter box," she muttered as much to herself as Chase, disappointed at forgetting such a critical piece of cat care. "My neighbor has cats. I'm going to call her and see if she has a setup I can borrow. Are you okay in here?"

Chase nodded, not taking his gaze from the animals. He seemed adorably fascinated by them. No wonder all those kitten and puppy firefighter calendars sold so well. It was an appealing combination.

"I'm fine. Stella texted and asked if she could go back to one of the girls' houses and watch a movie. I told her to be home by ten thirty. I have a feeling she's going to wish she'd come earlier when she gets a load of these two."

The kittens were daintily walking around the laundry room, investigating their new surroundings.

"I'll be back shortly," she told him with a nod and turned for the kitchen.

Chapter Fifteen

Chase walked through the dark house toward the laundry room, enjoying the quiet. He rarely slept more than four or five hours a night, even at his own home, but he'd dreaded being awake when he was on his own.

For some reason, the silence of his empty home had been louder than a shattering scream. It was part of why he built his studio on the property. He needed a way to occupy himself and did a lot of his work in the middle of the night.

He didn't feel that same restlessness in Starlight. When they'd first arrived and the pain plus his usual demons woke him, he would sit on the sofa in Madison's family room and turn on the Christmas tree lights, breathing in the pine-scented air and the peace that her home gave him.

The same calm she helped him access, even though he didn't deserve it. On the nights Madison spent in his bed, he'd had no desire to leave her warmth.

Even when sleep eluded him, it had been enough to listen to her breathe, her presence relaxing him more than any pill or potion.

He imagined she was fast asleep upstairs. There had been little chance of her coming to him, not with how angry she'd been after discovering he'd given her number to his doctor. He hated the idea of her going out with Marcus Wiley, but couldn't she see that he was doing her a favor?

It had been nearly midnight before he'd convinced Stella to go to bed once she got home. Madison had walked upstairs with her after they checked on the kittens one last time.

Note to self, Chase thought. If he ever made a woman really mad, a box of abandoned kittens worked as an effective distraction.

Now he eased open the door of the laundry room, wanting to check on their overnight guests. To his surprise, they weren't alone. Madison was curled up on a pile of blankets next to the bed she'd arranged for the strays. She looked up, her gaze gentle as she took him in.

"They're sleeping," she whispered, crooking a finger in his direction. He moved forward, thinking that he'd never seen a woman look more beautiful than she did with her hair streaming over the pillow and a bulky sweatshirt covering the top half of her body visible above the quilt.

The kittens were nestled in a furry ball against her chest. "I was worried, so I came down to check on them," she told him. "They're purring in their sleep."

"The tile floor can't be comfortable," he said. "Do you want me to take a shift watching over them?"

She smiled. "It's fine. I want to stay here for the night. I need to know they're going to make it."

He lowered himself until he sat next to her on the blanket. "I'm sorry I insinuated you weren't capable of taking care of them. I'm also sorry I gave Marcus Wiley your number."

"I understand," she told him, which quite possibly made him the sorriest. "You can lie down if you want." She lifted her head and pushed one of the pillows toward him.

"If you want to be alone…"

"I don't."

Neither did he. More importantly, he wanted to be with her. So he did what she said and stretched out next to her. She was sleeping on her side, and he faced her, not touching but close enough to smell the scent of her vanilla lotion.

He reached out to stroke a finger along the fragile nub of kitten backbone under the downy fur. Then his hand brushed Madison's. He interlaced their fingers, grateful beyond measure when she didn't pull away.

Maybe she would remember how angry she was tomorrow, and he certainly deserved it. For now, he was more than happy to enjoy this hushed truce.

Even though he knew it was impossible, Chase wanted a million more of these moments together.

And he wasn't a man given to wanting things that were so obviously beyond his reach.

Possibilities. That was what Madison represented for him. Possibilities were the most dangerous desires of all.

"You can't send them away," Stella pleaded the next morning. "Please, Madison. They belong here."

Madison bit down on her lip and tried not to let her emotions show on her face. "Those kittens deserve a good life, Stella. The animal rescue in town can help them find it."

"What could be better than the life we could give them?" the girl demanded, then turned her attention to the kittens. Chase had done a quick examination this morning after they gobbled down breakfast to determine they were both girls, and she'd named them Pip and Pop.

"You and your brother are returning to Seattle after Christmas," Madison reminded her. "And I work a lot of hours."

"But they have each other for company."

As if wanting to prove the girl's words true, Pip executed a spastic hop in the air and landed on her sister's back. The two slid across the hardwood floor as they wrestled, a tangle of black fur and white-socked feet.

Stella laughed, and even Chase grinned. It wasn't easy to remain unaffected by the kittens' cuteness.

Madison planned to drop the two animals at the animal shelter before she went to work that morning. She and Chase had spent the night sleeping on the laundry room floor, hands held, the kittens between them.

He confused her more than any man she'd ever met. What had started as a simple good deed for a floundering girl who'd lost her parents had turned into much more for Madison.

Was she indeed the only one who felt their connection?

She didn't want to believe it.

"Please. Can we keep them until Christmas?" Stella glanced at her brother. "Chase and I could adopt them. They aren't any trouble. I'll scoop poop and use my babysitting money to buy their food."

He ran a hand through his hair. "It isn't about the cost, Stel. Animals are cute when they're babies, but those kittens are going to grow into adult cats in no time at all."

"I like cats," Stella shot back. "It's not as if I'll want to dump them because they aren't little anymore. Who would be so cruel? I would love them and take care of them for always."

"That's a fine thought, but you don't know the first thing about taking care of animals."

"I had a goldfish once," the girl muttered.

Chase looked distinctly uncomfortable on the hot seat, and Madison suddenly understood that he was thinking more about his own capacity for taking care of something—or someone—than Stella's.

"I'll talk to the people at the rescue," Madison said into the ensuing, weighted silence. "I have a feeling Pip and Pop are too little to be adopted out right now. On the phone this morning, the woman mentioned they'd have to be spayed first, and they like to wait until animals are at least two pounds for that. It wouldn't be the worst thing if they let me foster them for a few weeks."

What in the world was she doing? She was less prepared to take care of kittens than Stella. Until recently, Madison hadn't been the type to rescue stray animals...or people.

Now she couldn't seem to stop herself.

"Thank you," Stella breathed and popped up to give Madison a tight hug, then sent a dark glare in Chase's direction. "Thank you for having a heart," she told Madison. "I'll go with you to the shelter so I can hear what they say about how to take care of them." Another pointed look at her brother. "*I* want to learn to be a good caregiver."

"Let's put them back in the laundry room for now," Madison said, doing her best not to look at Chase. "I have a few calls to make before heading to the shelter."

"You bet." Stella scooped up the kittens and headed for the laundry room. She grabbed her laptop from the counter. "I have one more school assignment to turn in before I'm officially on break. I'll sit with the kittens until you're ready to go."

As soon as the laundry-room door clicked shut, Chase rounded on Madison. "Are you trying to prove I'm a horrible person?" he demanded. "Nobody is debating you. It's an argument you don't need to have. You've already won."

Nothing about this moment felt like a victory. Madison's instinct was to snap back, to spit out some sarcastic remark or angry put-down. She was an expert at pushing people away with her anger, just like Chase. But she didn't want to anymore. She wanted something better for both of them.

It still felt ironic that she'd put herself in the position of bringing whatever light she could into his and Stella's lives. Madison had been described in a lot of ways, but *sunny* had never been an adjective associated with her. Even so, she had her own brand of warmth she could offer if he was willing to take it.

"I don't think you're a bad person." She moved toward him. "I think you've done great things in your life. You've overcome obstacles, and when Stella needed you, you stepped up. You didn't have to take care—"

"Of course I did. I was named in the will as her guardian. I had no choice."

"People always have choices, Chase. You made a good one." She lifted her hand to his cheek, her heart warming as he swayed into her touch. His eyes closed for a second, and his shoulders seemed to relax. She drew strength from their connection. He might want to deny it, but that didn't make it less true.

"There's no reason to think you won't continue to do the right thing," she continued, "if you refuse to let yourself off the hook. Stella belongs with you."

I belong with you, she added silently.

"You owe it to you and her to try." She needed him to be willing to try with her as well. "You've made huge strides here in Starlight and—"

"I'm meeting with my cousin next week," he said. When Madison would have pulled her hand from his face, he covered it with his. His eyes held so much distress. "She wants to talk about Stella and the future."

The news was like a knife to Madison's heart. "Have you told Stella? You have to talk to her first."

"I know what she'll say, but I also know what's best for her. It's not me."

She breathed out a sharp laugh. "Just like you know who I should date?"

"I should have told you before I gave him your number. He's a good guy, Madison. It kills me to think of you going out with Marcus. I want what's best for you. Both you and Stella. I can't be that for either of you."

He leaned in and pressed his forehead against hers. "No matter how much I want to."

How much could Madison push? How much did she have to give? What would it take for Chase to see he was wrong about himself and her?

About all of it.

"I wish you could see yourself the way I see you," she told him.

He sighed and then pressed his lips to her skin. The kiss was so gentle and tender it made a shiver run through her. "Me, too, sweetheart," he said into her hair. "Me, too."

"You live up to the hype."

Chase stopped sketching long enough to glance at the woman who stood in the doorway of the studio space he'd rented the following day in the Starlight Community Center. He recognized her as Cory Schaeffer, Madison's friend and the wife of Jordan Schaeffer, the Trophy Room owner and a former NFL football player.

Like most of the people he'd met in town, Cory and Jordan were nice people. Good people. The kind he wasn't used to being around.

"I haven't drawn this much in years," he said as he pushed a piece of paper across the table. "I'm rusty, so it's definitely not my best work."

"Let's not get all Braggy McBraggster that you turn out this level of work rusty," Cory told him with a wink.

Chase chuckled, then realized he needed to keep the conversation going. That was what normal people did. "Madison said…um…you're also an artist. You make jewelry or something like that. Crafty."

"Jewelry," she confirmed, her smile widening as she moved toward him. "Yes, I'm crafty and creative. Also artistic, although certainly nothing near your level."

"Huh," he muttered, trying to force himself to come up with another question.

"That was hard for you, wasn't it?"

He blinked. "What?"

"Making conversation. Asking me about myself. Social graces." Her tone was warm and teasing, like someone's favorite teacher.

"Yes, but it isn't polite for you to point it out. According to Madison, you're the mom figure in your group of friends."

"Call it tough love, then. Your mom never tried that?"

He placed the piece of chalk he held onto the table and grabbed a towel to wipe his fingers. "My mom didn't try much of anything other than complaining about how I cramped her style. She had aspirations of being a star. An unplanned pregnancy and a kid weren't part of the plan." Why was he sharing so much with this stranger? Once he'd started talking, he had trouble forcing himself to stop.

Cory inclined her head. "I'm familiar with bad parenting. That's why I'm glad I had the chance to do something different for my son. I would never want him to feel the way my mom made me feel."

"Does everyone carry the burden of their childhood into adulthood?" Chase wondered out loud.

"I think in some manner," Cory said. "But then we choose the kind of adults we want to be, so that works out for some people."

"But not everyone," Chase answered.

"Not everyone," the woman conceded. "Madison is determined that it will work out for your sister."

He nodded. "Stella's been through a lot, but she had parents who loved her before the accident took them from her. I'm going to make sure she has every opportunity for a happy life."

"That's a gift," Cory said. "I wonder if it's one you can give yourself?"

"What has Madison told you?" He didn't like to think of his struggles available for public consumption.

She shook her head as she picked up one of his drawings. "No specifics, which shouldn't come as a surprise with her. We can tell she likes you."

"She'll get over that."

"Will you?"

"I don't matter," he said, then held up a hand. "I'm not looking for you to change my mind. It's a fact."

"I don't know if your sister or Madison would agree, but I'm not trying to convince you. However, I do want to mention that if you're looking for a fresh start, there's no better place than Starlight to find it. That's why I came to find you today. There's a guy who lives about five miles outside of town, an artist with his own workshop. He mostly does metal work, although the studio is also piped, so you could put in a furnace. His wife called me because he was recently diagnosed with early stages of Alzheimer's."

Chase shook his head. "It's a horrible disease."

"Yes, it is," Cory agreed. "They're moving to Arizona, where their son and daughter-in-law live. She called to see if I knew anyone who would be interested in taking a look at the property. I thought of you."

Chase did not appreciate the quick swoop his heart did in response to her words. He ruthlessly tamped it down. "Why would you think I'd be interested? I live in Seattle."

"I grew up in the Midwest," she said. "That didn't make it my home. I found a home when I came here. It wasn't easy, but it was worth the challenges."

"Did Madison tell you that the orthopedic surgeon from the hospital asked her out?"

Cory frowned. "She didn't mention a doctor."

"I gave him her number."

"Are you dumb?" Cory blurted, then shook her head. "Don't answer that."

Chase smiled. "Despite what she may think or what anyone may think, I care about Madison. Dr. Wiley is a good guy. The type of guy I'd want for my sister or—" he lifted a brow "—a friend I cared about."

She held up a hand. "I get what you're saying. Just keep in mind what I said about that property. Christmas is next week. You and your sister and Madison should concentrate on enjoying the last bit of the season. I hear you have quite a way with the kids in the choir."

"You hear a lot," he told her.

"Enough," she agreed. "It was good to talk to you, Chase. I like your art. I like you, and I can see why Madison does, too. Think about what I said."

"I will, but it won't change my mind."

Nothing would.

Chapter Sixteen

Madison drew in a deep breath and turned away from the stove in the Seattle youth center's kitchen.

"Could you talk to him tonight? Help me think of a way to convince him sending Stella to live with his cousin in Portland would be the worst idea in the world? You have to see why it's essential that Chase change his mind."

Jenna's delicate brows winged down over her guileless blue eyes. Although the more powerful similarities came in their personalities, she and Chase's younger sister genuinely looked like they were related. Stella was sweet with a huge heart, just like Jenna had been as a kid.

They may have had different upbringings, but that

only gave Stella more of an advantage, to Madison's mind. It also made the girl more vulnerable. Madison had done everything she could to protect Jenna from the harsh realities of their life when they were little kids, but there was no hiding all of the unfortunate details of how they were raised.

Stella had a good family, parents who loved her, so it was even more critical that Chase understand how much he meant to his sister. Who better to explain that than Jenna, who'd been disappointed and let down and nearly killed by Madison?

"Why are you so invested in Chase and Stella Kent?" Jenna asked, handing Madison a pan of lasagna.

Madison placed it in the oven along with the other three trays, then closed the door and set the timer. In addition to prepping food for the community meal at Trophy Room, she'd also made food for the holiday celebration at her sister's after-school program.

She, Chase and Stella had driven into the city earlier that afternoon. She'd dropped them off at Chase's house before picking up her sister to start the prep.

Chase and Stella, along with some of the other teenage volunteers and their families, would join them later to help serve program participants.

"I'm not invested. I'm just helping."

"I don't understand why," Jenna said, shaking her head.

"It's an extension of what I do for you." Madison

shrugged. "I know I haven't been able to make it in for my cooking class, but I'll be back in the New Year."

"It isn't the same, Madi. You met that girl less than a month before her brother's accident. She was practically a stranger. Chase *was* a stranger, and yet you invited them into your home. I thought it was some sort of misguided guilt from our accident, like you could fix them the way you hadn't been able to fix me."

Madison took a deep breath, forcing back the regrets that tied her to her sister. "Nothing could make up for the guilt I feel over what happened to you. I stole your future."

"The accident took away my ability to have children," her sister said calmly. "I'm still here, and I'm okay. Better than okay."

Madison picked up a sponge and wiped a small splatter of tomato sauce from the counter, unable to meet her sister's gaze. "I don't believe you. I can't. You and David would be the perfect parents, but because of me—"

"We're going to be parents." Jenna grabbed her hand, but Madison had trouble hearing her sister around the sudden rush of blood in her head.

"Do you mean…?" She glanced at Jenna's flat stomach.

"I'm not pregnant. Medicine can do a lot, but I'm not ever going to be pregnant. David and I have been approved to become foster parents. Today, we got word that two girls, eight and fourteen, are being placed with us next week."

"You wanted a baby," Madison insisted. Remorse pinged through her, deflating her limbs with its sharp edges.

"Dreams change," Jenna told her. "You should understand that. David and I want a family. A home with kids in it—laughter and tears and slamming doors."

"A teenager, Jenna. Why?"

"You know why. What would have happened if that horrible social worker hadn't made it clear she couldn't find a home for the two of us together?"

Madison shrugged. "I was never going to be placed in a home, not a decent one."

"I couldn't enjoy life without you," Jenna said. "We didn't want the same thing to happen to these sisters. As soon as I heard about them, I knew they were right for us. In my heart, I knew it."

Madison dropped the sponge and reached out to pull her sister forward. "You're a good person, Jenna. The best. These girls have no idea how lucky they are."

"Stella Kent is lucky because of you," Jenna countered. She drew back. "Is it possible she should go live with this cousin? I met Chase when she was referred to the program. He did not seem equipped to handle a teenager. It didn't surprise me she acted out, and it wouldn't surprise me if it happened again once they return to Seattle."

"Come on." Madison shook her head. "You can't believe that. I'm helping him realize that he has more to offer than he understands. He's doing the work."

Her sister smiled. "I know you, Madi. You always do the heavy lifting. Your love language is acts of service done with an attitude."

"Your psychology degree mumbo jumbo is lost on me," Madison said, rolling her eyes.

"I have a teaching degree, as you well know."

"Stella belongs with Chase." Madison said the words with all the conviction in her heart. "Just like you belonged with me. I wish I would have found a way to keep us together."

"Let's not forget that you were also a kid."

"This isn't about me."

"For me it is." Jenna reached out and squeezed Madison's hand. "You hide your heart, Madi. But it's big, and I don't want you to be hurt if Chase Kent refuses to live up to your expectations."

Madison appreciated her sister's concern, even if she didn't want to need it. "Then help me make sure he does."

Chase wasn't sure why it had taken him so long to see the truth about Madison. Now that he recognized it, he couldn't focus on anything else.

When they first met, he'd thought they were similar. He'd dismissed their connection, making the excuse that she was just as broken and soulless as he was, which made them feel like they were on the same team.

He hadn't understood what made her willing to go out of her way to help Stella and, tangentially, him. Two weeks of proximity with Madison winding her way past his defenses like a cool breeze had made it clear.

She had a huge heart and a boundless capacity to protect the people she cared about. Her hard shell didn't hide a heart that was two sizes too small. There was no hiding because she was all heart, even though she would deny it.

And if she was all heart, was it possible she might have a piece of it to spare for him? Enough to help him out of his self-imposed emotional exile. If a woman like Madison thought he was worth saving, didn't he owe it to both of them to try?

Possibilities.

They terrified him.

As they served food to the crowd of teenagers and adults, Chase was fascinated watching Madison's interactions with the kids and their families, if they had family members with them.

"She keeps close to the food because it's a shield for her."

He turned to Madison's sister, Jenna, who'd come

to stand next to him. "A pan of lasagna will keep her safe from people?"

She arched a delicate brow.

"Yes, I see what she does. The food is an expression of her caring. She doesn't need to depend on it, though. Your sister has plenty to offer outside of the kitchen."

"I think she's slowly coming to see that. After she got sober, it took a while for her to trust that she wasn't going to ruin anything or anyone she came into contact with."

"You topped that list."

The younger woman's mouth tightened. "I never felt that way."

"Even after the accident?"

"How much did Madison tell you?"

"Enough."

The woman seemed to consider that. "Do you blame Stella for the explosion and fire in your studio?"

"No."

"It's probably similar."

"I blame myself."

Jenna coughed out a laugh. "Or not."

"If I had given Stella more attention or the right kind of affection, she wouldn't have needed to befriend the losers who led her down that negative path. We're going to fix it. Fix her."

"You and my sister have more in common than

I realized. You both control everything about your lives. What's it like to have that kind of power?"

He thought for a moment about how to answer, then said, "Overwhelming and heavy."

She patted his arm, a gesture reminiscent of Madison. "You've got this. Madison has faith in you, and she's an excellent judge of character."

If only Chase could feel so confident. He began to clean up as some of the dinner guests finished. Jenna said a few words to the crowd and credited their full bellies to her sister. Madison blushed at the round of applause she earned for providing the food.

She did not take a compliment well, which endeared her to him all the more.

"How's it going?" he asked Stella as he joined her in the kitchen rinsing dishes.

"Do you ever think things happen for a reason?" She looked up at him with innocent gray eyes.

He didn't allow himself to believe in fate or have faith in anything outside of his power to make things happen.

Overwhelming and heavy, for sure, but he also didn't want to burst whatever bubble his sister had created in her mind. She was young. She deserved to believe in something bigger than herself, especially after everything she'd been through.

"I think it's possible," he answered.

"I don't mean like my parents' accident." She frowned

as if she were worried he might think she'd altered her view on the moment that defined her young life.

"That was a senseless tragedy," he agreed.

"But what if I was meant to get caught with the beer and fireworks at the school?" She turned to face him fully.

"Don't make excuses for your mistakes."

"I'm not. It was wrong, and I dealt with the consequences a lot better than my so-called friends. Their parents just signed off on most of the community service hours we were assigned. They didn't have to do any real volunteering."

"Then they also didn't learn any real lessons other than relying on Mom and Dad to snow blow for them."

Her forehead puckered. "I think you mean snow-plow."

"Right. Whatever it's called, those boys would have benefited from being held responsible for their volunteer hours the way you were."

"I agree." Stella shifted onto the balls of her feet, leaning forward like she was communicating something of great importance. "It was here that I met Madison, and that's changed everything."

Chase felt his breathing falter. Yes, Madison had changed everything, and not just for his sister.

"A Christmas miracle," he murmured. "But I'll deny it if you tell Madison I said so."

Stella shrugged. "She'd deny it, too. I was worried

Joey and Hunter might show up tonight. You never told me if you're going to go after them for messing around in your studio."

He'd given a lot of thought to his options and talked to Parker Johnson, Josh's brother and attorney who used to live in Seattle, about what it would mean for himself, Stella and the boys if he pressed charges.

"They're out of your life," he told his sister. "That's my silver lining in this whole mess. I'm not going to take action against them as long as you stay away from both boys."

"About that…" Stella worried her bottom lip.

"Don't tell me you're going to try to see them. No, Stel. I thought you'd learned your lesson."

"I don't want to see either of them ever again," his sister promised. "But I'll have to when I go back to school."

"I suppose." He rubbed a hand over his jaw. "We could—"

"Unless we stay in Starlight," she said on a rush of breath.

Chase took a step back, so shocked it felt like a feather could knock him on his butt.

Twin spots of pink had risen to Stella's cheeks, and her breathing turned shallow. He could tell she was nervous suggesting this, but it didn't make her stop.

"Think about it. Your studio needs to be rebuilt anyway. Why not rebuild in Starlight? I like it there.

You like it there." She leaned in and gave him a penetrating look. "You like Madison."

"She's helped us a lot," he said like that explained it.

"I saw you two kissing the other night on the sofa." Stella made a face. "It was gross, but it's okay with me if you want to date her. If you want to stay in Starlight, I want to stay in Starlight."

"We can't," he answered without thinking.

"Why?" He recognized the slightly petulant tone that crept into her voice. "You don't have friends in the city, and we agree my friends are a bad influence."

"Make new ones," he told her, taking another step back.

"I have in Starlight. What's stopping us?"

"Seattle is my home. It's your home."

Her eyes immediately filled with tears. "I haven't had a home since my parents died. We could start over in a place where I'm not the weird orphan girl."

"People will hear about your background anywhere," he argued.

"I've already told most everyone I've met in Starlight," she countered. "They don't look at me like I'm a freak. I feel like I belong there. You do, too, Chase. I can tell."

Two other volunteers entered the kitchen at that point. "Bad time?" the dad asked, placing an arm around his preteen son's thin shoulders.

"It's fine," Chase said, forcing a smile before returning his gaze to Stella. "Can we talk about this another time?"

"Yes, but I don't want to go back to my same school after Christmas. I need something different, Chase. Something new. I'm not the only one."

He thought about his cousin and how Stella would react to the news. Maybe her desire to leave Seattle would help pave the way for her to accept that there was something better out there for her.

Or maybe he could do what she asked.

He'd thought about a million different scenarios in his head. Still, amid all those possibilities, the thought of actually staying and making his home in Starlight had never crossed his mind. Perhaps when Cory Schaeffer mentioned the studio coming on the market, but that didn't count.

That hadn't included Stella.

Chase might not believe he deserved a chance at happiness, but his sister did. He'd thought his best option was sending her to Portland with his cousin, but what if there was another choice for both of them?

Stella suddenly tipped her head at the sound of singing coming from the youth center's main room. "They're singing Christmas songs." She tugged on his hand. "The rest of the dishes can wait. Let's go show off our Kent pipes."

He smiled as he followed her, then paused.

Stella glanced over her shoulder. "What?"

"Did you hear that?" he asked. "I swear I just heard bells ringing."

"Your imagination," his sister told him and pulled him forward again.

Maybe, he thought. Or perhaps he did believe in miracles after all.

Chapter Seventeen

"Why are you giving me that look?" Sophie asked as she grabbed the ladle from Madison's hand two nights later. "I thought you wanted to find a good home for the kittens."

"I do." Madison's stomach knotted with unease. "I don't think they're ready yet. They're too little."

"My friend talked to the people at the rescue. She has to sign a contract to promise to have them spayed once they reach two pounds. As long as she does that, the adoption manager said she can have them for Christmas."

"I know," Madison said through gritted teeth. "The rescue called me to tell me the good news."

"You don't look happy about it." Sophie frowned. "You said you didn't want to keep them."

"I don't." Pip and Pop had been with Madison for less than a week, but the two little creatures had burrowed their way into her heart just as surely as they snuggled in their bed of pillows.

She hadn't allowed herself to contemplate adopting them permanently, but she wasn't ready to let them go.

It was selfish, but the idea of another family adopting the furballs made her throat tighten. She cleared it and looked at her sous-chef. "I hoped Chase would reconsider adopting them for Stella."

That was only partially true. Madison hoped Chase would first reconsider his decision to send Stella to live with his cousin and then agree to keep the kittens.

"Just say the word, and I'll tell Mischa she has to find another perfect Christmas gift for her kids."

Madison nearly groaned out loud. She couldn't be selfish. If she wasn't going to keep Pip and Pop, and Chase was unwilling to entertain the idea, she needed to let the kittens go.

She needed to let Chase and Stella go as well.

But her heart couldn't bear the thought of it.

She swallowed back her overarching fear of commitment. "I'm keeping them," she told Sophie.

She half expected her employee to be angry, but Sophie threw her arms around Madison, who offered a stiff pat on the back.

"Oh, my gosh," Sophie said. "You're getting better at hugs. It used to be like hugging a porcupine. Now you're more like a hedgehog."

"Thank you. I think that was a compliment."

"It's a step in the right direction. Just like you keeping the kittens. You realize I was making the whole thing up about my friend?"

Madison felt her mouth drop open. "You're fired," she said when she regained her composure.

"Those kittens were meant to be with you, just like Stella and her hottie brother. I believe in Christmas miracles."

"I'm going out on a date with a doctor next week," Madison said. "Coffee on Christmas Eve. A doctor who Chase set me up with."

"A love triangle—that's even better."

"It's not a love triangle. Why would he set me up? He doesn't want to date me. I can't handle a relationship. I'm not sure I can handle kittens. They should find someone else to take them."

"They're yours." Sophie shook her head. "They all belong to you, whether you know it or he knows it."

Tanya Mehall, Trophy Room's longtime bartender, poked her head around the kitchen's swinging door at that moment. "Madison, your guy is here," she said. "And there's a bachelorette party with a lot of tipsy bridesmaids."

"He's not mine," Madison said, even though her

gut clenched at the thought of another woman touching him...kissing him.

"He looks like he needs rescuing just the same. The poor guy is going to have to start wielding his cane to beat them off."

"Get out there, Chef," Miles told her.

"He's not mine," she insisted.

"Then be a friend, at least." Sophie came forward and untied Madison's apron, pulled it over her head and shoved her toward the swinging door.

Madison glared over her shoulder. "If this is all the fake setup like the kitten story..."

"Go," Miles and Sophie said at once.

She tugged her hair out of the ponytail she'd been wearing since early that morning and stepped into the crowded bar.

She saw several groups of locals she knew and waved. Then a gaggle of boisterous women at the far end of the bar drew her attention.

Tanya hitched her head in that direction as if Madison needed the coaxing. Chase was smiling at one of the women, but he looked ten kinds of uncomfortable.

As he looked up, his gaze crashed into hers. At the same time, one of the women draped an arm over his shoulder and pressed against his side.

She pushed her breast into him, and Madison suppressed a laugh when his eyes widened with alarm.

She quirked a brow.

Help me, he mouthed.

She thought about turning around. Madison didn't owe anything to Chase. He'd given out her number to another man, after all.

But it didn't matter.

Sophie had been right. Jenna was right.

He belonged to her.

She wanted to belong to him.

She moved toward him, ignoring the greetings of people who tried to talk to her. Madison had recently started coming out from the kitchen each night to interact with customers and friends. It was a considerable change in attitude from when she'd first moved to Starlight, but tonight an even more significant shift was taking place inside her.

One that allowed her to finally choose the life and love she wanted without worrying about what it would mean if he didn't want her back.

"Excuse me," she said as she elbowed her way through the bachelorette party.

"Do you mind?" one of the women snapped. "We're standing here."

Madison stopped and gave the woman a look meant to eviscerate without words. She knew it would penetrate even a gallon of liquid courage. "You're in my way."

The path immediately cleared.

Chase swiveled on the bar stool, and she stepped between his legs, the heat of his body warming hers.

"Took you long enough," he told her quietly.

"I know." He was talking about the seconds she'd wasted watching the women flirting with him before coming to his rescue. She was talking about so much more.

She lifted her hands to his face, loving the feel of his stubble scratching her palms. Loving him, even though she wasn't quite ready to reveal that much.

But this was a claiming, and she wouldn't back down.

She leaned in and kissed him, pressing her lips to his in a slow, deliberate savoring. No one could mistake the message she conveyed to Chase and everyone who watched the scene unfold.

She registered his surprise as he stilled, and Madison realized he could end this before it started. She hadn't needed to go this far in her gesture. There were subtler ways she could have let his pack of admirers know he was off-limits.

Then his arms came up and around her, pulling her even closer. Their breath mingled as he met her halfway in the intensity of the kiss. A thousand sparklers lit inside Madison's heart.

He was claiming her in return. That was how it felt, and she refused to believe it could be anything less.

The whistles and cheers that ensued barely registered in Madison's foggy brain. All she felt and saw and cared about was Chase.

"Thank you," he said when he drew back—only inches—a few moments later.

Out of the corner of her eye, she saw that the bachelorette party had moved toward the back of the bar. Her heart gave a little stutter. Did he think this was just for show? That she'd made such a public declaration simply to save him from a bit of aggressive flirting.

"For not giving up on me," he continued, and her heart seemed to settle. "You matter, Madison."

"I do," she agreed. "You do, too. To me. To Stella."

His steely gaze clouded. "I don't want to hurt either of you, but "

"It's almost Christmas, Chase." She lowered her hands to his arms and squeezed. "Let's enjoy this time."

"You kissed me in public," he said, as if her whole body wasn't tingling with euphoria already.

She wanted to say the words. *I love you. You're mine, and I want to belong to you in return.*

Something held her back. Baby steps, she reminded herself. This was new territory for them both.

Instead of saying anything, she leaned in and kissed him again.

"I can't do it."

Chase placed a hand on Stella's trembling shoulder. "Of course you can. You know the song backward and forward. Your voice is incredible, Stel. You're going to be amazing."

She shook her head. "I'm too nervous."

They stood together backstage at the Starlight high school auditorium where the holiday concert was taking place. Chase had trouble reconciling this version of Stella with the teenager he'd come to know over the past couple of weeks.

The one who was confident and charismatic, a complete one-eighty from the sullen, shy girl who had come to live with him after her parents died.

How could a couple of weeks change so much? Was it just the magic of the holiday season, like some twinkle light–decorated smoke and mirrors mirage?

Now he faced another version of his stepsister, one he had little understanding of how to deal with. He wasn't good at pep talks, motivational speeches or anything that involved being a role model.

"What about those Kent pipes you've been displaying during rehearsals? Tessa picked you for a solo because you're good, Stella."

The girl bit down on her lower lip. "She picked me because she's friends with Madison, and I'm the girl who doesn't have parents."

"Good point," he admitted.

"Chase, oh, my God. You're not making me feel better."

Right. "It doesn't matter why she picked you. What you do with the opportunity is what counts."

"And if I puke all over the audience?"

He shrugged. "It won't be the first time most of

those old people have seen vomit." In addition to friends and family, the crowd included residents from the area's assisted-living centers and other locals. The auditorium was packed full.

She coughed out a startled laugh. "Is that the best you can do?"

"I believe in you," he told her honestly. "Does that help?"

"Yeah." She drew in a deep breath. "It actually does."

"Channel your inner kitten," he said, thinking of Pip and Pop. "They have no fear, and Pip has gotten quite vocal."

"You said this morning that listening to her meow makes you think she got her tail caught in a door."

"You can't do any worse," he said, chucking her on the shoulder.

"You're awful at this." Stella shook her head but looked less nervous than a few minutes ago. Maybe he'd done his job after all.

"You'll be great," he repeated.

"Stella, you're almost on," Tessa stage-whispered from near the curtain's edge.

"I'll be right here." Chase gave her a cheesy thumbs-up.

Stella gave him a quick hug. "Thanks, Chase. I'm not sure what for, but thanks for being here."

"Sure, kid."

He pressed two fingers to his chest and rubbed at

the dull ache as she hurried forward. Tessa dropped a kiss on Stella's head and whispered something that had the girl nodding.

Of course, the caring redhead would know what to say. Hell, even Madison knew how to speak to Stella and make the girl feel comfortable. Everyone around him seemed more capable than Chase. He did nothing but fail each time he tried.

Words failed him. The right actions failed him. Maybe not when he and Madison were alone at night—his body had no trouble communicating with hers—but he knew that wasn't enough.

He wasn't enough, no matter how much he wished he could be.

"Chase?"

He turned at the sound of his name and then did a double take. "Brandie, what are you doing here?" He'd looked up his cousin online, which was how he recognized her so quickly.

She offered a gentle smile as she stepped forward. "You asked me to come, remember?"

He blinked, then glanced toward the stage. Stella was walking forward for her solo. He didn't want to miss it, but he couldn't ignore his cousin until Stella finished her song.

The last thing he needed was for her to realize his plan before he'd finalized it. He knew how mad she'd be and how angry Madison would be on Stella's behalf. As much as he would like to believe he could

change enough to be the type of guardian his stepsister needed, he didn't know how.

"You haven't told her yet," Brandie said, a subtle
admonishment clear in her soft tone.

Chase shrugged. "I thought it was better if we
met first. If it doesn't work out, I don't want to get
Stella's hopes up for nothing."

He frowned as he cocked an ear toward the front
of the auditorium. "As you can see and hear…" He
paused to listen to his sister's clear voice ring out
from the front of the stage. "My sister—"

"Stepsister," Brandie corrected.

He gave a reluctant nod. "She's as sweet and
funny as she is talented. She's not going to give you
any trouble."

"So she doesn't take after you?" Brandie asked
with a chuckle. She was about six years older than
Chase, the only daughter of his father's older sister.

They'd only met a couple of times growing up.
In fact, Chase's mother made sure he remained connected to his father's small family since Martin had
wanted little to do with his son.

"She does not take after me," he confirmed.

"It was a joke, Chase," Brandie told him. "I raised
two boys. I'm not afraid of a spot of trouble. I know
precious little about you other than your reputation
as an artist."

"There's not much more to me. Nothing of conse-
quence, which is why I appreciate you considering

this arrangement. Stella needs someone with experience who knows how to be a mom or a parent. She drew the short end of the stick when she got stuck with me as her guardian."

Brandie gave him a funny look. "I saw that hug she gave you. She doesn't seem to mind."

"Kids are resilient. Most creatures are. If I'm all she has, then this is what she knows—like a wire monkey. She deserves better." He glanced toward the stage again. "Can we talk in more detail at breakfast? I don't want to miss the whole performance."

"I'd like to meet her," Brandie said. "We don't have to tell her what's going on yet, but I'd like to see how she reacts to me and get to know her."

That had not been part of his plan for this visit, but he couldn't very well deny his cousin the request. Brandie and the girl should get to know each other if this was going to happen before the start of the next school term.

An uncomfortable tightness settled in the pit of Chase's stomach, but he told himself he was doing the right thing. He needed to stop kidding himself into believing he could make this work.

The longer she was with him, the worse he knew it would be when he messed up again. They'd had some near misses—the incident at the school, her running away and the explosion in his studio. What would come next?

Possibilities had been consuming him lately, but

he didn't want to consider the potential outcome if things went wrong.

"I'll bring her tomorrow," he said. "We'll tell her you're in town for the day and wanted to meet both of us. Dad should have done a better job of staying in touch with his family. Things will go as they should after the holiday."

"I'm going to watch the rest of the performance from my seat in the audience," Brandie told him with a nod. "I'll see you tomorrow."

Chase turned back and hurried over to stand next to Tessa at the edge of the curtain.

"She's amazing," the woman said, nodding her head toward Stella as she came to the end of the last stanza of "O Holy Night."

"Yes, she is," Chase agreed.

His gaze strayed to Madison, who sat in the front row beaming with pride. She would hate him after this, but not as much as he hated himself.

Chapter Eighteen

Madison left the house before sunrise on Christmas Eve to start initial preparations for the community supper at Trophy Room and because she didn't want to talk to Chase the morning of her date with Marcus.

She'd thought about canceling a dozen times in the past few days. There was nothing she wanted to do less than go out with another man when Chase Kent held her heart.

But she was following through on the date. Maybe the self-destructive aspect of her personality led the charge—the part she thought she'd left behind when she'd given up her vices.

Maybe she wanted to go out with the man Chase thought was more appropriate for her to prove that she knew best. Although she hadn't previously trusted her heart to lead her in the right direction, it did know best.

She'd arrived at the restaurant in the cold and dark before sunrise, but by the time she entered Main Street Perk a few hours later, the town was bursting with last-minute holiday excitement.

She had a new appreciation of Christmas magic. After everything that had happened and the shifts in her life during the past couple of weeks, how could she not believe in miracles?

She'd dressed today in a festive red sweater and her favorite ripped jeans. Her evolving wardrobe was a reflection of her new outlook. Sure, she still preferred blacks and neutrals, but she was slowly adding in pops of color. Stella had helped her pick out this sweater on their trip to Spokane.

Instead of feeling like a lemming going along with the pack wearing holiday-themed colors, Madison felt like part of the community in a way she hadn't let herself before.

Marcus sat at a table near the back of the coffee shop and waved when she came in. He'd texted her ten minutes earlier to ask what kind of drink she preferred, so she joined him at the table instead of heading to the counter.

"It was nice of you to get my coffee," she said as she sat down.

"Not a big deal," he told her. "You look very pretty and in the holiday spirit today."

"Thanks." Heat crept into her cheeks. It would be difficult not to be affected by a compliment from a man as handsome as Marcus. He wore a dark gray sweater, jeans and the same boots from the night of caroling. But all the compliments in the world wouldn't change the fact that Chase Kent held her heart and didn't even know it.

"Are you ready for Christmas?"

She nodded. "I am, or I will be after tonight. I'm helping to serve the holiday supper my boss hosts at Trophy Room every year."

"Did you cook for the event?"

"I've been cooking for weeks. Today is all about prep and making sure everything gets and stays warm simultaneously."

Marcus made a face. "I'm embarrassed to admit I've been known to mess up boiling water." His mouth curved at one end. He really was an attractive guy and would make a great catch for some lucky woman, just not Madison.

"If it makes you feel any better, I would botch a surgery. I was terrible at science, although I'm pretty handy with a knife."

His smile widened. "Good to know."

They talked for a few more minutes, and Madison cursed her self-destructive streak. She didn't want to use this man to make Chase jealous or spur him into action. She liked Marcus, just not the way he obviously liked her.

"Oh, no. What did I do?"

Her gaze darted to his. "What do you mean?"

"You have a look on your face like somebody gave you bad news."

"Not exactly, but am I that transparent? I've been told I have a pretty good poker face."

"Whoever told you that must have been on the other side of the poker table from you."

She nodded. "I'll keep that in mind. I appreciate the coffee, and I appreciate everything you did for Chase. Ella wasn't lying when she said you're a good guy."

"I sense a huge *but* coming my way."

"But I've recently met someone, and it would be unfair to you to let this go any further."

"He's a lucky guy, whoever he is," Marcus said.

She wondered if Chase would consider himself lucky. Madison kept her features purposely blank. It wouldn't be the smartest thing for her to admit that the guy who'd essentially set them up was the man she liked.

"The nurse Chase hires to take care of him after the next surgery will have big shoes to fill."

She blinked. "His next surgery back in Seattle," she supplied carefully. She didn't want Marcus to realize that he'd revealed something about a patient she didn't already know because she knew he wouldn't tell her any more.

And right now, she needed to know more.

"I guess it makes sense that he's choosing to have it there." Marcus lifted and lowered one broad shoulder. "I offered to do it, but since he didn't want to stay in Starlight for the recovery... I'm not as willing as his doctor there to let him go to somebody else after. I like to see my patients through until they heal fully."

"But he needed to get back to Seattle." She processed the words in her own mind. "That makes sense because Stella will be starting school."

"Yes, Chase should have his sister settled in Portland by then."

"With his cousin," Madison murmured, feeling as if her world and everything she thought she knew to be true about her relationship with Chase—the connection she'd come to believe in with her whole heart—was turning inside out.

Stupid, stupid heart.

"It had to be a huge help to Chase to have your help during his recovery. You're a good friend, Madison. Whoever this man is you've started seeing is a lucky guy."

Marcus smiled at her gently. "If things don't work out between the two of you...give me a call, okay?"

Madison nodded, her mind reeling. Chase had given his doctor the impression that she was part of why he'd decided to send Stella away? How could that be possible when it was the exact opposite of what she wanted?

Unless her neediness had made it painfully clear to Chase he didn't want that kind of commitment in his life.

He'd warned her, and she'd fallen for him anyway.

Despite what Marcus Wiley thought, Madison possessed an incredible poker face. What else could get her through the remainder of their date with a smile on her face?

She managed to hold up her end of the conversation even though her heart felt like it was shattering inside her chest. And when she finally bade the handsome doctor goodbye, wasn't it just her luck to see Chase walking into the coffee shop with Stella and another woman?

Based on the shocked look on his face when he saw her, she knew exactly who the older brunette with her hair styled in a functional bob was.

How could he do that to his sister on Christmas Eve?

One of the baristas stopped her to talk, and she waved to Marcus as he exited the shop. Madison answered the questions about the timing of the community supper and then started to leave, her stomach turning over like a brick had been dumped in it, when Stella spotted her.

"Madison," the girl called even as Chase shook his head and said something to his sister that had her frowning.

Oh, no.

Whatever was going on with Chase, he wasn't about to turn Madison into the bad guy in this situation. She'd made plenty of mistakes, but this debacle rested solely on his wide shoulders.

She approached the table with a smile, confident Chase could read the fire snapping in her gaze as she looked at him.

"Hey, guys," she said. "Merry Christmas Eve. Sorry I missed breakfast this morning. I needed to get to—"

"Were you on a date?" Stella demanded, her winged brows lowering over those gray eyes.

Madison blinked. This was Chase's method for putting distance between them?

"More like coffee with a friend," she said calmly.

Stella looked pained as her gaze darted from Madison to Chase. She shifted closer to her brother like she suddenly needed to protect him.

Sweet, unknowing girl.

"This must be your cousin Brandie." Madison held out a hand to the middle-aged woman. "I'm Madison Maurer, a friend of Stella's."

"It's nice to meet you," Brandie said. She was the type of woman who gave off maternal vibes like a thousand-watt amp. Madison couldn't stand her on principle.

"You're visiting from Portland?" Madison asked.

"We shouldn't keep you from the preparations for tonight," Chase said.

"Yes," Brandie answered. "I wanted to meet Stella. Chase has told me so many wonderful things about her."

The girl looked even more confused as she studied her brother. "You did?"

"Portland is a great city," Madison said. "Wonderful schools." She turned to Stella. "I have a couple of friends who run a farm-to-table restaurant downtown. I'll arrange to visit them, and hopefully, you'll have time to see me, too."

Chase might not want her in his life, but he would not—could not—force her out of Stella's.

Madison registered the change in the girl's demeanor, despite her anger and heartache, and suddenly realized she'd spoken out of turn.

Madison had been so intent on her feelings about Chase's choices that she hadn't realized Stella might not fully understand why this random cousin had suddenly shown up.

The girl's breathing had gone shallow. "What do you mean?" She turned to her brother. "Chase, what is she talking about? Why would I be in Portland?" She placed a hand to her heart as her gaze settled on Brandie. "Are you here to take me with you?"

Stella's chair scraped across the coffee shop's concrete floor as she pushed back from the table.

Chase immediately stood and reached for his sister, although she yanked away from his grasp. "Brandie is here to meet you and have an initial conversation about the future. Nothing more."

His gaze swung to Madison, who glared at him. "This is none of your business," he told her.

If Chase had expected her to be cowed by his tone, he should have known better. Her shoulders went stiff as her chin tipped up in defiance.

"You are a coward," she told him. "I deserve better than you throwing a man in my path like chum in the water. Stella deserves better than you making plans for her future as if she has no say in it."

"Stella, would you like to come live with me in Portland?" Brandie asked.

The noise that came from his sister's throat would have broken Chase's heart if he believed he had one.

"Stella, it's for your own good. I want what's best for you."

"You want what's easiest for you," his sister shot back. Tears streamed down her face, and seeing what his actions had done to her made him feel like each drop of moisture was a spike shoved under his skin.

"You have to understand." He shook his head, unsure how to explain something he didn't understand. Before he could puzzle out a response, Madison wrapped an arm around Stella's trembling shoulders.

"Come on, sweetheart. It would help if you had

time to process this. It will be okay. We'll figure it out."

"You are not a part of this," he blurted before thinking better of it, then immediately regretted the words.

The depth of pain that flashed in Madison's eyes before she masked it was almost his undoing. His sister didn't bother to hide her feelings on the matter.

"You're such a jerk," she told him. "No wonder Dad didn't want anything to do with you."

Just when Chase had convinced himself he was the only man alive who didn't possess a heart, his broke as he watched the two women who were most important to him in the world walk out of the coffee shop and away from him. They were together, and he was left alone.

Again.

Only not quite alone.

"I assume that didn't go anywhere near how you planned it," his cousin said as she mopped a hand across her brow.

"Not exactly." He lowered himself into his seat. He would have liked to stalk out after Madison and his sister but was afraid his legs were too weak to carry him, and not because of anything to do with the accident. He could feel the stares of the people surrounding him, and his neck burned as much from personal shame as public humiliation.

He usually didn't care one whit what people thought of him, but now he did. Now he couldn't help it because this town had become his home in only a matter of weeks.

He'd ruined everything.

"Why did you agree to let me meet Stella without her knowing the potential plan?"

He placed his head in his hands. "I thought the decision would make more sense once she met you. You're better suited to raise a teenager—particularly a girl—than I could ever be."

"And what of your friend Madison?"

"I would not say we're friends."

"I'm certain she would agree at this point." Brandie lifted the coffee cup to her mouth. "But I was married once, and I've raised children who have fancied themselves in love. I know the look. Anyone can see the connection that pulses between the two of you."

"You heard her," Chase said miserably. "She was here on a date."

"That you set up." Brandie shook her head. "You know, my mother used to talk about your father. Her obstinate, controlling brother. She said he refused to accept happiness as his right and overcomplicated things or made excuses to stay miserable because that made him most comfortable."

"He found happiness eventually with Stella's mother." Chase drummed his fingers on the table. "At least, I think he did. I don't know what kind of internal demons tortured him, but his life was better once I wasn't a part of it."

Brandie looked confused. "He was proud of you."

"He hated me," Chase said with a laugh, although the sentiment didn't feel the least bit funny.

"No. My mother died three years ago. Up until that time, she and your father corresponded regularly. She enjoyed writing letters longhand, and he would respond in his sloppy, curt writing style. She treasured those notes. Often, he sent clippings of articles that featured you or printed photographs of your latest pieces."

Chase shook his head as his world tilted yet again. "From the start, my father had nothing but contempt and disdain for my chosen path. It was shamefully, woefully embarrassing for him to have an artist as a son, even one who was commercially successful. Nothing was enough. I invited him…" He cleared his throat. "He received invitations to every one of my openings but never once attended."

"Maybe not some grand party," Brandie conceded. "Your dad was a simple man, but he went to everything, based on the pictures he sent Mom. He was proud of you."

It seemed nearly impossible to believe, although Chase knew his cousin had no reason to lie to him. "I embarrassed him."

"He wasn't embarrassed by you. Why would he have named you Stella's guardian if he was ashamed?"

Chase swallowed, his throat suddenly parched. "That is something I've been trying to work out since the moment she came to live with me. It didn't make sense. I assumed he was arrogant enough to believe he'd never need me in that capacity. As if putting me in the will was some sort of cruel joke."

"I don't think it was a joke. I know what you and I have talked about as far as Stella's future, but in light of everything—"

"No. I am not fit to care for her. She deserves better." She was not the only one. Brandie could do a better job than Chase ever would.

"You're wrong about this. Stella seems like a lovely girl and is clearly loyal. She is not afraid to stand up for what she believes in. I admire her spirit. The two of you have some things to work out. No matter what the final decision is, I'm glad we connected. I want to stay in touch with both you and Stella. My boys are grown. Like I told you, I don't have a lot of other family."

"I don't have any family," he said.

Brandie shook her head. "You have Stella. Don't lose sight of that."

"You saw what happened. I'm not sure I can make it better. She might be thoroughly through with me."

"People make mistakes, Chase. What are you willing to do to fix them?"

If only he could believe it was that easy. If only he didn't suspect that this mistake was the best outcome for Stella in the end. She would want to get away from him, and if he finally admitted what was in this heart he resented possessing, that wouldn't change his penchant for self-destruction.

He refused to take down the people he cared about in the process. He said goodbye to his cousin and walked out into the cold morning. The town sidewalk bustled with people, and he could see the lights already on across the street at Trophy Room.

Madison and her friends would be there getting ready for tonight's supper. He pulled his phone out of his pocket and checked the app that helped him track Stella's location. She was at the bar as well. It was the best place for her, surrounded by Madison and her friends. So where did that leave Chase? He looked down at his injured leg.

It wasn't as if he could easily make an escape. He wasn't even allowed behind the wheel of a car. He needed to get away from the things he wanted but couldn't let himself believe he was worthy of having.

Time and space, that was what he needed. The time and space to figure out what came next. He glanced up to the sky as snow began to fall in fluffy flakes. Then he put his weight on the cane and started down the sidewalk alone.

Chapter Nineteen

By the time the bulk of the volunteers arrived at Trophy Room for the Christmas Eve community supper, Madison had been on her feet for nearly eight hours. The plan had been for her to take a break in the afternoon before returning to the bar to help serve the meal, but she'd needed to be busy.

She'd also wanted to stay away from home, knowing that Chase could potentially be there. Eventually, she'd insisted Stella allow Tessa to drive her to the house. The girl had been distraught at the events that had unfolded earlier in the coffee shop.

Madison shouldn't have been surprised. Chase had given her every warning he'd never veer from the path they'd started on when they first met.

She'd naively assumed that the changes inside her would be met with matching changes from him. She thought they were in this together, but now she was alone because that was how it had always been. Her friends rallied around her, but it did little to ease the ache in her chest.

She'd allowed herself to believe that Chase and Stella belonged to her, that she'd finally found her people—the ones who would help make her whole.

She'd denied she cared about that for too long, and now it was too late.

"Are you going to let him stay?" Ella asked. They were setting out trays of salad and bread. The volunteer servers had begun to mill about the bar, and festive music played in the background.

Cory and Ella had come in a few hours earlier to help decorate. They'd hung paper snowflakes from one end of the bar to the other and added festive potted poinsettias to the regular and high-top tables. Madison had spent enough years drinking to know that Jordan was losing money by closing the bar on Christmas Eve but was grateful he chose to.

She needed this reminder right now—sharing in the hope and joy of the season, even if hers had been dashed.

"I won't kick Stella out," she said, because discussing the girl was easier than revealing her complicated and unwanted feelings for Chase.

"Even if the man who broke your heart is part of

the deal?" Ella muttered a curse. "On Christmas Eve, no less. A real piece of work, that one."

Madison shook her head and started to deny her broken heart, but why should she? Her friends knew her well enough to recognize the truth.

"I don't hate him. That's the strangest part. I'm angry, but mostly I feel sorry for him. He honestly believes he has to take these drastic measures. It's not about Stella. She's an excuse. It's about how much he has to dare to give if he stays. I wish it were different, but I'm not fool enough to think I could change who he is as a person."

"Would you if you could?"

Madison thought about Ella's question. "No. Chase is the man I fell in love with. While it might have been stupid on my part, I don't regret it. I regret how it's ending, but..."

"I hate him for you," Ella said as her eyes narrowed. "And it looks like I may have the chance to kill him."

Madison glanced over her shoulder to see that Stella and Chase had come into the bar with the most recent group of volunteers. Stella immediately headed toward Brody and the group of teenagers clustered near the jukebox, which left Chase standing on his own.

Word traveled fast in a small town. Although Madison didn't consider herself popular in Starlight the way Tessa or Cory was, she was a local. This was her home, and small towns took care of their own at the end of the day.

"You've got to talk to him," she told Ella. "He looks so uncomfortable. It's going to make Stella feel weird and…"

"What if I offered your words back to you? It's not about Stella." Ella gave a wry smile. "We both know that's the truth."

"I would say you don't know what you're talking about and to mind your own business," Madison answered without hesitation but with no heat in her voice because Ella was right. "I can't talk to him right now."

"But you still want me to?" Ella shook her head. "I don't like how he treated you, Madi."

"Me neither," Madison admitted. "But this is me being the bigger person. I could give lessons on how to be a mature adult."

One of Ella's delicate brows rose. "Let's not push it."

Madison hugged her friend—still awkwardly—then headed back to the kitchen while Ella went to speak with Chase.

"I heard he's here," Sophie said as she bent to take another lasagna pan out of the oven. They'd made enough food to feed at least a hundred people, and Madison hoped it would be enough. She hoped this supper would remind the people attending that they weren't alone—the same way she wanted Chase to understand that.

"You want me to dump hot coffee on him?" Miles asked as he poured himself another cup. Madison's Christmas gift to her staff had been a new coffee maker in the kitchen.

"Of course not." Madison wondered exactly when she'd matured enough not to want to lash out at someone who'd hurt her. Maybe she truly had changed for the better.

She leveled a stare at her line cook. "I don't think you should be drinking coffee this late in the day, either."

Miles laughed. "I'm good until at least ten, although I haven't been sleeping well lately, now that you mention it."

"We'll switch to decaf in the afternoon," Madison told her employees. "There are too many side effects from all that caffeine."

"You sound maternal," Sophie said, her mouth agog.

Miles nodded. "It's freaking me out. You should yell at me or call me a doofus."

"I've never used the word *doofus* with either of you," Madison insisted.

Sophie and Miles shared a look.

"Yes, because you used far worse language." Miles thumped his palm against his forehead. "Even your language is changing. Chase Kent might be a world-class jerk, but he and his sister have certainly influenced you—in a positive way."

"You fight for the good ones," Sophie said.

Madison was suddenly more tired than she'd ever felt. "I'm sick of fighting. First for myself and my sister. Then fighting my demons—against myself because I couldn't believe I deserved to be in my own corner. Even here in Starlight, I fought to keep myself at a distance. I understand what Chase is doing. It's easier to be a jerk than to risk his heart, but I don't want to fight with him."

"What about *for* him?" Sophie asked quietly.

"Is it bad to say that I want somebody to fight for me for once?"

Sophie moved around the counter and hugged Madison. "Still reminds me of a hedgehog," she said. "But you're not wrong for wanting that."

Cory stuck her head into the kitchen and announced they were ready to start serving. Madison and her staff brought out the final dishes, and pretty soon she didn't have time to think about fighting or her broken heart because she was so busy serving food and talking to people. The dinner was another fundraiser for the Starlight community center, and the event was a big success from the start.

Whole families arrived together, some of them clearly in their church clothes. There was a mix of older and younger members of the community. Even though small talk was Madison's least favorite activity, especially on this particular day, she found herself laughing and smiling.

Eventually, fatigue took over, and the socializing became too much. She retreated to her kitchen, where there was plenty of work still to do. It was good to have something to keep her occupied.

A moment later, the swinging door opened and Chase walked in. For a few seconds, the noise of the crowd filled the silence. Then the space went quiet as the door closed once again.

"I owe you another apology," he said by way of greeting. "I should have told you about Brandie."

Madison blew out a breath. She must truly be on the brink of exhaustion, because the anger that had coursed through her earlier was gone. All she felt was a deep sorrow when she looked into his eyes.

"You did tell me. I thought these past few weeks had changed things."

"Perhaps they did," he agreed.

"Yet you're having a second surgery and didn't bother to mention it."

His mouth tightened. "There are a few things that aren't healing right, according to Dr. Wiley. But I've imposed on you enough."

She moved her hand between the two of them. "Is that what you think this was? You were an imposition to me?"

"I think I can't be who you need."

"Can't or won't?"

"Does it matter?"

She laughed at the truth of his words. "Not really. How's Stella?"

"Angry with me, but she'll eventually understand this is for the best."

Just when Madison thought her heart couldn't break any more, he said something like that. "There's nothing about what you're doing that's for the best. Don't kid yourself into thinking there is."

He looked at the floor. "We're going back to Seattle tomorrow."

"On Christmas Day?"

"I think it's the right choice, given everything that's happened. If you want me out of the house tonight, I understand. I arranged for a driver tomorrow because I know Stella will want to celebrate Christmas with you in the morning."

"Stella doesn't want to leave Starlight."

"I can't give her that option."

"Can't or won't?" Madison muttered, then shook her head. "I don't blame you, Chase."

"Because a snake can't change its nature?" he offered.

"You're a good man. I still believe that, even if you won't let yourself. I fell in love with you knowing exactly who you are." She pulled on the apron string, worrying the thin piece of fabric between her fingers. "I fell in love with you because of who you are."

His mouth gaped open, and she could tell she'd shocked him. "Don't tell me it comes as a surprise to you."

"It's not how this was supposed to go."

"That doesn't mean it's not right. I wish you could see that, but at least you showed me I'm worth more than I thought. It took you not daring to open your heart to realize that I could give mine to someone. Even though it hurts, I don't regret it. But I promise that you will regret it if you let Stella go."

"I can't even begin to tell you the things I regret," he said, his voice so desolate that Madison wanted to reach for him.

She didn't, and after a moment, he walked out again.

"I don't understand why you're being so hateful," Stella said as the black SUV rolled out of Starlight.

"I'm trying to do the right thing." Chase ran a hand through his hair. "Why won't anyone believe that?"

"Because it's wrong for us to leave Madison on Christmas."

"She has the kittens and her friends," he said. "It isn't fair of me to stay there, Stella. I'm hurting her."

"You're hurting yourself most of all," his sister shot back.

"Old habits," Chase said quietly. He glanced at the driver in the front seat, but the man kept his eyes on the road ahead. The driver he'd hired was getting paid a small fortune for working on a holiday and braving the roads after it had snowed almost five inches in the past twenty-four hours.

The driver, who was based out of Montrose, had texted Chase early that morning, unsure whether the mountain pass would be drivable, given the winter conditions.

"I'm sorry for saying that Dad hated you," Stella said after a few minutes.

They were slowly making their way to the top of the mountain pass. The valley below was a perfect winter wonderland scene with snow blanketing every tree branch and ice crystals glistening in the pale sunlight. Chase wished his heart—the one he claimed not to have—could be as frozen as the view out the darkened SUV windows.

He turned to his sister. "It's okay, Stella. Dad and I never got along. I know you were lashing out in anger, and I don't blame you. Neither of us needs to pretend that—"

"He was in awe of you," she interrupted. "And kind of jealous, I think."

Chase thought about his cousin's words in the coffee shop yesterday. Was it possible that his certainty about his father's animosity toward him was actually unfounded?

"He said you thought you were better than us because you never came over for dinners or holiday celebrations."

"He never invited me." Chase had scheduled his deadlines so that he was busy around the holidays. Every holiday. He never wanted a free moment, because that might remind him of how alone he truly was.

Stella shrugged. "I don't know why, because he seemed mad you weren't around. But he told me that you had more intelligence and creativity in your big toe than he did in his whole body. He used to play the lottery every week, and he'd say that if he won, he would buy a Chase Kent original."

Chase cursed, and Stella sucked in a breath. "He didn't need to buy one. I would have given him whatever he wanted if I'd known he felt that way. It wasn't like that when I was growing up. He was mean and cruel on the few occasions when I saw him."

It felt ridiculous to reveal that to his younger stepsister, but Stella's revelation about his father gutted Chase.

"I think my mom was good for him," Stella said. "She was good for everybody." The girl sniffed. "I miss her. I miss him, too. He wasn't perfect. We weren't a perfect family. I don't want perfection, Chase. Who cares about fresh baked cookies when I come home from school?"

"Seriously?"

"Well, they would be nice, but it's not like that's

what's most important. I'm not a baby. I get how things work. I get that you want to have your life back. I'm a huge imposition. Please don't pretend like you're doing this for me. Being sent away isn't what I want."

"It's what I wanted growing up," Chase told her, then grabbed the door handle as the car skidded around a corner. "Everything okay?" he asked the driver.

"Yeah," the man answered. "I thought everything was clear, but it was icier than I expected at the top of the pass. I'll take it slow, chief. No worries."

Chase hoped he could trust the man and suddenly questioned the wisdom of hiring a driver who was willing to work on Christmas Day. Yes, the money was good, but it had been slim pickings in the ride-share app. Maybe he should have taken that as a sign. There were so many signs he'd ignored.

"I don't know what to do to make it better for us, Stella. I'm scared I'm going to screw it up worse, so giving you the kind of guardian I wanted seemed like the smartest option."

He lowered his voice as he studied his sister. "I'm scared of what could happen. I'm terrified you're going to wind up pregnant or in a drunk-driving accident. Or who knows? There are awful things that happen in the world. You know predators target girls on those apps you love so much."

"I'm smarter than that, Chase."

"I'm not," he said. "I have no idea how to deal with raising a teenage girl. It isn't because of my lifestyle. It's because I don't want to fail you. I still can't quite believe your mom and my dad made me your guardian. I want to do a good job for you, but I don't know how. I hate not knowing what to do."

"You just have to be there," she answered like it was that simple.

"You have to be there, too," he countered. The girl frowned. "I mean it, Stella. You can't shut me out and go to your room and lie and sneak out. This parenting thing is not for the faint of heart."

She flashed the barest hint of a smile. "I think that's why Dad trusted you. He knows you're stubborn and pushy, just like him."

It was the strangest compliment Chase had ever received. "Do you really not want to give Brandie a chance? She'll take good care of you. You could be happy with her."

"I think I could be happy with you."

Chase felt warmth spill through him, and he pressed his hand against the SUV's window to ground himself with the cold. There was no use continuing to deny he had a heart, because it throbbed in his chest with fear and exhilaration.

Could they make it work? He wasn't sure but figured he owed it to Stella and himself to give it a try. "We're going to go to therapy," he told her, eliciting a groan. "It's nonnegotiable. Also, you're not going to hang out with those same losers from the high school parking lot. Promise me."

She nodded. "Would you consider going back to Starlight?"

"Right now?" He swallowed.

"I wouldn't be opposed to now, but I mean for good."

"It's not my home," he said more out of fear than believing that. He'd messed things up with Madison and couldn't imagine returning to Starlight if she wasn't a part of his life.

"It could be. Tell her you're sorry."

He didn't pretend to misunderstand whom Stella was referring to. "I'm not good at apologies."

She rolled her eyes. "But can you try?"

"Excuse me, John?" He tapped the driver on the shoulder.

"Yeah, chief?"

"Change of plans. Instead of going all the way to Seattle, I need you to take us back to Starlight."

"That cuts a lot of time off the trip," the man said as he navigated another curve on the windy mountain road. "I'm missing Christmas dinner at my mom's house for this money, so…"

"I'll pay you the same amount," Chase assured the driver. "Maybe you'll be able to make the dinner after all."

"Your call, then." The man flipped on his signal

even though they were the only vehicle on the road and began to make the turn.

Suddenly the car lurched as they hit another patch of ice. Stella screamed, and Chase instinctively shot out an arm to hold her back even as the SUV went over the side of the mountain.

Chapter Twenty

Madison looked around the home filled with her friends and tried to remind herself how lucky she was to have found her place with these amazing people who loved her.

Years ago, when her life was nothing more than vacillating between an obsession with work and drinking to forget her past, she never could have imagined how good things would be. She silently chided herself for the deep sorrow she felt after saying goodbye to Stella and Chase that morning.

He'd been right all along. She was the one who'd changed their deal. He'd never promised her anything, and she'd tried to fool herself from the start that she wouldn't want something more.

The funny thing about making her life better was that she had a taste for the possibility of embracing the future with an open heart, so she couldn't go back to being satisfied with less. The old Madison would have holed up in her house, steadfastly rebuilding the walls around her heart and reminding herself why she needed to cut herself off from caring.

She now realized that while alone might be easier, it wasn't what she wanted. Pushing people away would not make her heart ache less. She'd accepted Ella's invitation to join them for Christmas dinner because food was more than paying tribute to the ingredients in a recipe. It was about sharing part of herself with the people she loved.

In addition to Ella, Josh and his daughter, Anna, the group included Tessa, Carson and Lauren, along with Cory and Jordan and their son, Ben. Josh's mother had come from Spokane for the holiday, and his brother, Parker, and Parker's wife, Mara, and her daughter, Evie, who was Anna's best friend, were also there.

Ella's father was supposed to stop by later, and Madison realized she took comfort in being around people despite her sadness. Maybe she'd visit Stella when she returned to Seattle to volunteer at the youth center. She didn't think Chase would forbid the girl from seeing her or Madison would visit the teen in Portland if she went to live with her cousin.

Madison hoped that wouldn't be the case. Chase needed Stella, even if he didn't realize it. Madison liked to think he needed her as well, but that was another ending to the story, one it was clear she wouldn't get.

A Christmas tree held pride of place in the corner of the family room, colored lights twinkling as the kids watched the train that circled the track Josh had built under the tree. Madison would leave soon, returning to her quiet house—although not lonely with Pip and Pop waiting to keep her company.

When the doorbell rang, and Ella moved to answer it, Madison didn't pay much attention, assuming it would be someone joining the party. She was still smiling at the kids when she realized a hush had fallen over the room.

She turned to see Ella staring; her friend's face had gone stark white. That was when she noticed Nick Dunlap. He wasn't in his police chief uniform, but she could tell that he was there on official business.

Ella gestured for Madison, who walked forward with a vague sense of panic skittering across her nerve endings. She couldn't figure out what Nick would want from her.

Then Ella grabbed her hand. "You need to get to the hospital," her friend said in an urgent whisper. "There was an accident up on the pass."

Madison shook her head, still not understanding.

"A car went over the side," the police chief explained. "The passengers were Chase and Stella Kent."

Dots swam across Madison's vision as blood roared in her head.

"They're at the hospital." Ella quickly placed an arm around Madison's waist.

"Both with minor injuries," Nick added quickly. "Sorry, I should have mentioned that part first."

"You think?" Madison drew in a deep breath, trying to calm her thundering heart.

"I'll drive you," Ella said, but Madison shook her head.

"You have a house full of holiday guests. I'm fine to drive."

"I'd be happy to give you a ride," the police chief offered. "Or at least an escort."

"Everything okay?" Josh asked as he stepped into the entry.

"Fine," Madison said before Ella could answer. For some reason, she wanted to see Chase and Stella before word of the accident got out.

She saw her friend nod in agreement. "I'll be right there," Ella told Josh, then turned to Nick. "Make sure she gets to the hospital safely."

"I can take care of myself," Madison said automatically.

"I know," Ella assured her. "But you don't have to." She gave Madison a quick hug. Then Madison grabbed her coat from the hook where she'd hung it and followed Nick Dunlap outside.

"I really am happy to drive you."

"I'll be fine. Thank you." Madison shivered against the frigid air despite her puffer coat. "I'm fine now. As long as I know Chase and Stella are going to be okay."

He gave a curt nod. "That was the report I got. I haven't seen them for myself."

"I'm sorry you were pulled away from your holiday celebration." She stopped on the sidewalk in front of her parked car. "Why did you come to find me, anyway?"

"One of my deputies called and reported the accident," he said. "You were the person Chase Kent asked for at the hospital. My wife figured you'd be at Josh's since you're friends with Ella."

Madison nodded, trying to wrap her mind around Chase asking for her. "Thank you again."

"Let me know if you or they need anything. We'll get the vehicle towed into town once the conditions improve. I don't know what they were doing on the mountain in this weather, especially on Christmas Day."

Escaping her, she thought, but she didn't say it out loud. Even if Chase's summons didn't mean what she hoped, it wouldn't change Madison's choice to leave the Christmas gathering and rush to the hospital. Chase and Stella were her people. She'd learned a lot of lessons over the past couple of weeks, but one of the most important was that she showed up for her people.

The hospital was quiet as she walked in, which she figured was a blessing. Hopefully, Stella, Chase and their driver, if he'd been injured, had been seen and treated right away. No one should have to spend Christmas in the emergency room. She approached the desk and asked after the two Kents.

The receptionist flipped through files. "Mr. Kent has been taken to surgery."

"What do you mean surgery?" Madison demanded, leaning forward and pressing her palms on the cool countertop. "I thought his injuries were minor."

"I can't give you that information," the woman said, bristling. "I shouldn't have mentioned the surgery," she added under her breath.

"Where is Stella?" Madison glanced around wildly as if she could summon the girl with her worry. "Is she okay? What were the injuries? What can you tell me?"

"There are strict rules about patient confidentiality," the woman said. "Are you the girl's mother?"

Madison didn't hesitate. "Yes, I am. Please tell me where she is."

"Do you have identification?"

"I want to see Stella." As Madison's voice rose, the woman stood.

"Ma'am, I'm going to have to ask you—"

"Madison, is that you?" a voice called from the hallway.

"Stella!"

The receptionist looked over her shoulder and,

after a moment, gave a resigned nod. "I'll buzz you in," she said. "Miss Kent is in room eight."

Madison hurried through the door and down the hall. A nurse greeted her at the doorway of room eight. Another was helping Stella back into bed.

"She almost ripped out her IV trying to get to you," the nurse said, speaking to Madison. Madison's heart seemed to settle slightly as her gaze roamed over Stella. The girl had a cut above one eyebrow, and her wrist had been casted, but her color was good, and she looked to be in one piece.

She gave Madison a watery smile. "Merry Christmas. You thought you could get rid of us so easily."

The nurse appeared satisfied that Stella was settled in again and stepped away from the bed. Madison rushed forward and threw her arms around the teenager. Sophie would have been proud of her for this hug, because she gripped Stella like she would never let go.

"What happened? Are you okay? Where's Chase?"

The girl sniffed and swiped at her cheeks. "Our driver was a doofus," she said, using one of Madison's favorite monikers. "He was trying to turn around, and we slid off the road."

"Did the car flip?"

"Only onto its side." The girl shook her head. "There was about a ten-foot drop and then it leveled out again before pitching over the side. Luckily, we stopped. If we'd gone over all the way..." She shuddered. "It wouldn't have been good. I landed weird on my wrist. The doctor says it's just sprained, but then Chase had to get me and the driver out. The driver hit his head, and he was unconscious. We didn't know if the car was steady or not. It was kind of scary."

"It sounds terrifying." Madison's voice shook at the thought of the two people she loved so much in that situation. "I'm glad you're safe, sweetheart."

Stella tried to smile again, and then her face crumpled. "Chase had to break the glass, and his leg is messed up again. I guess it was already messed up, but Dr. Wiley took him back to surgery. Chase told them to call you so I wouldn't be alone."

Madison tried not to let disappointment curl around her ankles like some sort of insidious weed. Chase didn't want her for himself. He needed her for Stella.

"I'm here for you," she told the girl, because that was the truth. She left out the part of the truth where her heart was breaking all over again and reminded herself this was how it had started.

"I'm glad." Stella pressed her rosebud lips together. "I was scared, Madison. I started thinking about my parents and their crash and—"

"You're okay." Madison pulled Stella close again. "I'm here. Chase will recover, and you're going to be fine. That much I know for sure."

She was Stella's person, if not Chase's. For now, the girl needed Madison, and that would be enough.

* * *

Chase blinked awake slowly. His mind felt fuzzy like he was trudging through a thick pea-soup fog to put his thoughts in some sort of coherent order.

Images crashed through his mind. The white winter landscape spinning as the SUV slid across the patch of ice. Then the tumbling and Stella's terrified face as they went over the side of the mountain.

He should not have been on that road with her in those conditions, but that was a failure he could put aside for the moment. The white walls and ceiling of the hospital room were just as stark as the landscape on the pass, but he was warm.

Safe.

Stella was safe.

His leg was bandaged from midthigh to just under his knee. There was no pain at the moment, thanks to the IV drip attached to his arm.

He'd welcome the pain when it came because it meant he was alive. He could feel, and there was no more denying his emotions or the love he had in his heart for his stepsister and for...

Glancing at the empty chair in the corner of the room, he wondered if Madison had come to be with Stella.

He'd made the request, knowing he had no right to ask it of her.

Wanting her to come to their rescue once again.

The door opened, and his stepsister peeked in. "You're awake," she breathed.

"I'm good," he answered, knowing he needed to hear the words as much as Stella did.

To his eternal surprise and gratitude, Madison followed her into the room.

"You need to be more careful when pulling people from a flipped car," she said, one side of her mouth pulling up the slightest bit.

"Not planning to make a habit of it." He straightened on the bed and adjusted the thin gown he wore, suddenly feeling far too exposed.

Vulnerable.

"Dr. Wiley said the surgery went well," Stella reported as she came to sit next to him on the bed. All of her earlier anger seemed to have been forgotten.

A brush with death could do that for a person.

This was Chase's second since the holiday season started. What a way to celebrate Christmas. But if he needed a miracle, he'd gotten one today.

The miracle of realizing what a fool he'd been.

"How are you?" he asked his sister, placing a gentle hand on the cast that encircled her right forearm.

"I'm good, too," she said, sending a shy glance toward Madison, who continued to stand on the opposite side of the room.

She was here, at least. That was a start.

"We have a lot to talk about, Stella."

"Are you changing your mind from earlier?" She looked panicked at the thought.

"No. I'm not sending you to live with Brandie." He leaned forward. "Even if you beg me to go. You're stuck with me, kid. Sweet sixteen. Embarrassing prom photos. College visits. I'm here for all of it, no matter what."

Her wide grin made his chest clench. "What about school plays and choir concerts? I was thinking of getting back into that stuff."

"You bet. I'll buy earplugs in bulk if I have to," he said with a wink.

"So funny." Stella rolled her eyes dramatically, but she was still smiling.

"Excuse me?" A nurse poked her head into the room. "There's a boy in the waiting room asking to see Stella. He has flowers."

"Brody," his sister whispered.

Chase raised a brow.

"I texted him that we were here."

"Go say hi, then. I like that kid okay."

"Me, too," Stella agreed, then popped up and hurried from the room.

"I should go, too," Madison said, her arms wrapped tightly around herself. She didn't move. "If you need anything—"

"You. I need you."

The smile she flashed was so sad it almost ripped him in two.

"I know," she agreed. "And I can help with whatever Stella needs. I'm still your friend, Chase. You're welcome to stay with me until you figure out—"

"I don't want to be your friend, Madison." He shook his head when her chin trembled. "No, I do. But not just your friend. I don't want your help." He squeezed shut his eyes for a moment, frustrated that he was stuck in bed, unable to pace or move or run away. Afraid he would mess things up all over again. He had to try regardless.

"I want you," he said gently and met her confused gaze. "I love you."

He heard the breath she sucked in at his words even though his heart was pounding in his ears.

"You do?"

"More than I've ever loved anyone or anything." He crooked a finger. "Come over here, Madi."

"You don't have to do this," she told him, taking a slow step forward. "I'll still help you even if that's all it is."

"I love you with my whole heart. The one I didn't think I possessed. I was a tin man, but you brought me to life. You showed me what it was like to be cared for and loved just the way I am."

She was close enough now that he reached out and laced their fingers together, drawing her closer until her legs brushed the side of the bed, and then he pulled her down to sit next to him.

"I'm sorry I hurt you. I'm stupid and scared and a coward, just like you said."

"I might have been a little harsh," she admitted.

He put a finger over her mouth. "You were right, but I'm going to do better. If you give me another chance, I will spend every day proving to you that I love you. I want to earn my place at your side."

She smiled now and gripped his face in her hands. "Don't you understand, you big doofus? You don't need to earn my love. I give it to you freely, Chase. I love you no matter what. For always."

"And forever?" he asked, and she nodded.

Suddenly, his heart wasn't pounding anymore. It had settled into a contented rhythm as soon as Madison touched him. She was his place, his home, his North Star.

"This year," he sang, pressing a gentle kiss to her mouth, "I'm giving my heart to someone special."

"I'll keep it safe," she promised, and he deepened the kiss, knowing this holiday season had given him the most precious Christmas miracle of all.

* * * * *

Don't miss these other heartwarming
Christmas romances:

Expecting His Holiday Surprise
By Jo McNally

Their Texas Christmas Match
By Cathy Gillen Thacker

Lights, Camera…Wedding?
by Laurel Greer

Available now wherever
Harlequin Special Edition
books and ebooks are sold!

COMING NEXT MONTH FROM

⬡ HARLEQUIN®
SPECIAL EDITION™

#2953 A FORTUNE'S WINDFALL
The Fortunes of Texas: Hitting the Jackpot • by Michelle Major
When Linc Maloney inherits a fortune, he throws caution to the wind and vows to live life like there's no tomorrow. His friend and former coworker Remi Reynolds thinks that Linc is out of control and tries to remind him that money can't buy happiness. She can't admit to herself that she's been feeling more than *like* for Linc for a long time but doesn't dare risk her heart on a man with a big-as-Texas fear of commitment...

#2954 HER BEST FRIEND'S BABY
Sierra's Web • by Tara Taylor Quinn
Child psychiatrist Megan Latimer would trust family attorney Daniel Tremaine with her life—but never her heart. Danny's far too attractive for any woman's good...until one night changes everything. As if crossing the line weren't cataclysmic enough, Megan and Danny just went from besties and colleagues to parents-to-be. As they work together to resolve a complex custody case, can they save a family and find their own happily-ever-after?

#2955 FALLING FOR HIS FAKE GIRLFRIEND
Sutton's Place • by Shannon Stacey
Over-the-top Molly Cyrs hardly seems a match for bookish Callan Avery. But when Molly suggests they pose as a couple to assuage Stonefield's anxiety about its new male librarian, his pretend paramour is all Callan can think about. Callan's looking for a family, though, and kids aren't in Molly's story. Unless he can convince Molly that she's not "too much"...and that to him, she's just enough!

#2956 THE BOOKSTORE'S SECRET
Home to Oak Hollow • by Makenna Lee
Aspiring pastry chef Nicole Evans is just waiting to hear about her dream job, and in the meantime, she goes to work in the café at the local bookstore. But that's before the recently widowed Nicole meets her temporary boss: her first crush, Liam Mendez! Will his simmering attraction to Nicole be just one more thing to hide...or the stuff of his bookstore's romance novels?

#2957 THEIR SWEET COASTAL REUNION
Sisters of Christmas Bay • by Kaylie Newell
When Kyla Beckett returns to Christmas Bay to help her foster mom, the last person she wants to run into is Ben Martinez. The small-town police chief just wants a second chance—to explain. But when Ben's little girl bonds with his longtime frenemy, he wonders if it might be the start of a friendship. Can the wounded single dad convince Kyla he's always wanted the best for her...then, now and forever?

#2958 A HERO AND HIS DOG
Small-Town Sweethearts • by Carrie Nichols
Former Special Forces soldier Mitch Sawicki's mission is simple: find the dog who survived the explosion that ended Mitch's military career. Vermont farmer Aurora Walsh thinks Mitch is the extra pair of hands she desperately needs. Her young daughter sees Mitch as a welcome addition to their family, whose newest member is the three-legged Sarge. Can another wounded warrior find a home with a pint-size princess and her irresistible mother?

**YOU CAN FIND MORE INFORMATION ON UPCOMING HARLEQUIN TITLES,
FREE EXCERPTS AND MORE AT HARLEQUIN.COM.**

HSECNM1122

HARLEQUIN
PLUS

Announcing a **BRAND-NEW**
multimedia subscription service
for romance fans like you!

Read, Watch and Play.

Experience the easiest way to get
the romance content you crave.

Start your **FREE 7 DAY TRIAL** at
<u>www.harlequinplus.com/freetrial</u>.